This book
belongs to

. . . .

TALES OF DRAGONS & MONSTERS

Compiled by Tig Thomas

Miles
KeLLy

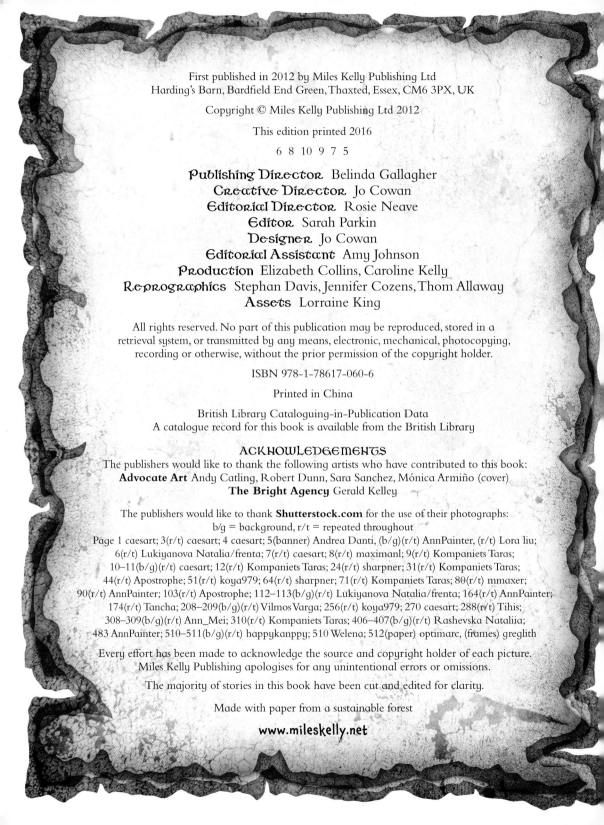

First published in 2012 by Miles Kelly Publishing Ltd
Harding's Barn, Bardfield End Green, Thaxted, Essex, CM6 3PX, UK

This edition printed 2016
6 8 10 9 7 5

Publishing Director Belinda Gallagher
Creative Director Jo Cowan
Editorial Director Rosie Neave
Editor Sarah Parkin
Designer Jo Cowan
Editorial Assistant Amy Johnson
Production Elizabeth Collins, Caroline Kelly
Reprographics Stephan Davis, Jennifer Cozens, Thom Allaway
Assets Lorraine King

ISBN 978-1-78617-060-6

Printed in China

British Library Cataloguing-in-Publication Data
A catalogue record for this book is available from the British Library

ACKNOWLEDGEMENTS
The publishers would like to thank the following artists who have contributed to this book:
Advocate Art Andy Catling, Robert Dunn, Sara Sanchez, Mónica Armiño (cover)
The Bright Agency Gerald Kelley

The publishers would like to thank **Shutterstock.com** for the use of their photographs:
b/g = background, r/t = repeated throughout
Page 1 caesart; 3(r/t) caesart; 4 caesart; 5(banner) Andrea Danti, (b/g)(r/t) AnnPainter, (r/t) Lora liu;
6(r/t) Lukiyanova Natalia/frenta; 7(r/t) caesart; 8(r/t) maximanl; 9(r/t) Kompaniets Taras;
10–11(b/g)(r/t) caesart; 12(r/t) Kompaniets Taras; 24(r/t) sharpner; 31(r/t) Kompaniets Taras;
44(r/t) Apostrophe; 51(r/t) koya979; 64(r/t) sharpner; 71(r/t) Kompaniets Taras; 80(r/t) mmaxer;
90(r/t) AnnPainter; 103(r/t) Apostrophe; 112–113(b/g)(r/t) Lukiyanova Natalia/frenta; 164(r/t) AnnPainter;
174(r/t) Tancha; 208–209(b/g)(r/t) Vilmos Varga; 256(r/t) koya979; 270 caesart; 288(r/t) Tihis;
308–309(b/g)(r/t) Ann_Mei; 310(r/t) Kompaniets Taras; 406–407(b/g)(r/t) Rashevska Nataliia;
483 AnnPainter; 510–511(b/g)(r/t) happykanppy; 510 Welena; 512(paper) optimarc, (frames) greglith

Every effort has been made to acknowledge the source and copyright holder of each picture.
Miles Kelly Publishing apologises for any unintentional errors or omissions.

The majority of stories in this book have been cut and edited for clarity.

Made with paper from a sustainable forest

www.mileskelly.net

Contents

SCALES AND TAILS

Boggarts, Trolls and Goblins

Gruesome Giants and Awful Ogres

WEIRD AND WONDERFUL BEASTS

TOOTH AND CLAW

SCALES AND TAILS

The Sea-Serpent

E Pauline Johnson

This tale is told by an old American Indian. He describes how one of his people became too fond of money, and how God, the Great Spirit, turned him into a terrible monster.

"Yes, it was during the first gold craze, and many of our young men went as guides to the white men far up the river. When the young men returned they brought tales of greed and murder back with them, and our old people and our women shook their heads and said evil would come of it.

"But all our young men, except one, returned as they went – kind to the poor, kind to those who were foodless, sharing whatever they had. But one, who was called Shak-shak (which means 'the Hawk'), came back with hoards of gold nuggets. He was rich like the white men and, like them, he kept it. He would count his money, count his nuggets, gloat over them and toss them in his palms. He loved them better than food, better than his life.

"The entire tribe arose. They said Shak-shak had the disease of greed. To cure it, he must give a great feast, divide his riches with the poorer people, share them with the old, the sick, the foodless. But he jeered and

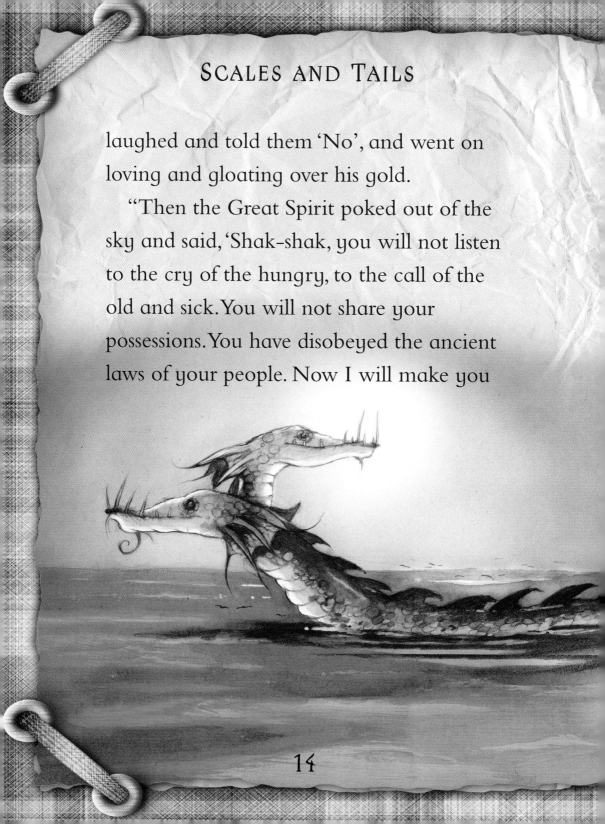

laughed and told them 'No', and went on loving and gloating over his gold.

"Then the Great Spirit poked out of the sky and said, 'Shak-shak, you will not listen to the cry of the hungry, to the call of the old and sick. You will not share your possessions. You have disobeyed the ancient laws of your people. Now I will make you into a thing hated by all men. You will have two heads, for your greed has two mouths to bite. One bites the poor, and one bites your own evil heart – and the fangs in these mouths are poison. Your evil heart will beat in the very centre of your foul body, and he that pierces it will kill the disease of greed forever from among his people.'

"When the sun arose the next morning the tribes-people saw a gigantic sea-serpent stretched across the surface of the waters. The tribes-people were stunned with horror.

They loathed the creature, they hated it, they feared it. Day after day it lay there, its monstrous heads lifted out of the waters, its mile-long body blocking all entrance to the sea. The chiefs made council, the medicine men danced and chanted, but the Serpent never moved. After the chiefs and medicine men had done all in their power, and still the Serpent lay across the waters, a handsome boy of sixteen approached them and reminded them of the words of the Great Spirit.

"'Let me try to find this evil heart, oh great men of my tribe,' he cried. 'Let me wage war upon this creature and try to rid my people of this greed.'

"The boy was brave. His tribes-people called him the Tenas Tyee (Little Chief) and

they loved him. He hunted food for the old
people, and he tanned skins and furs for
those whose feet were
feeble and whose
eyes were fading.

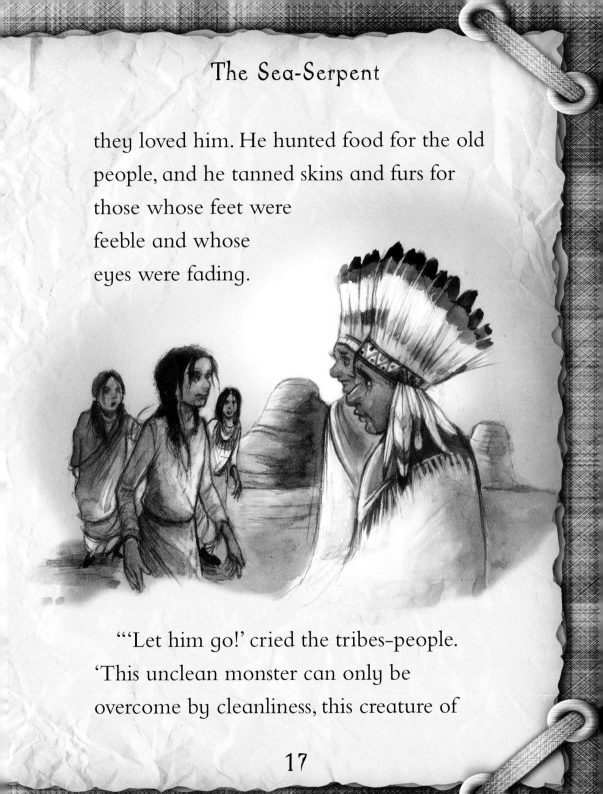

'‘Let him go!’ cried the tribes-people.
‘This unclean monster can only be
overcome by cleanliness, this creature of

greed can only be overthrown by generosity. Let him go!' The chiefs and the medicine men listened, then agreed. 'Go,' they commanded, 'and fight this monster with your strongest weapons – cleanliness and generosity.'

"The Tenas Tyee turned to his mother. 'I shall be gone four days,' he told her, 'and I shall swim all that time. I have tried all my life to be generous, but the people say I must be clean also to fight this unclean creature. While I am gone put fresh furs on my bed every day, even if I am not here to lie on them. If I know my bed, my body and my heart are all clean I can overcome this serpent.'

"'Your bed shall have fresh furs every morning,' his mother said simply.

The Sea-Serpent

"The Tenas Tyee then stripped himself and, with no clothing except a belt into which he thrust his hunting knife, he flung his young body into the sea.

"But at the end of four days he did not return. Sometimes his people could see him swimming far out in mid-channel, trying to find the exact centre of the Serpent, where lay its evil, selfish heart. But on the fifth morning they saw him rise out of the sea and greet the rising sun with outstretched arms.

"Weeks and months went by, and still the Tenas Tyee would swim daily searching for that heart of greed. Each morning the sunrise glinted on his body as he stood with outstretched arms greeting the coming day and then plunging from the summit into the sea.

"And at his home on
the north shore his
mother dressed his bed
with fresh furs each
morning. The seasons
drifted by, winter
followed summer,
summer followed
winter. But it was
four years before the
Tenas Tyee found
the centre of the
great Sea-Serpent,
and plunged his
hunting knife into
its evil heart.

"The Serpent

The Sea-Serpent

writhed, leaving a trail of blackness on the water. Its huge body began to shrink and shrivel. It became dwarfed and withered, until nothing but the bones of its back remained, and they, sea-bleached and lifeless, soon sank to the bed of the ocean. But as the Tenas Tyee swam homeward and his clean body crossed through the black stain left by the Serpent, the waters became clear and blue and sparkling. He had overcome even the trail of the Serpent.

"When at last the Tenas Tyee stood in the doorway of his home, he said, 'My mother, I could not have killed the monster of greed among my people had you not helped me by keeping one place for me at home fresh and clean for my return.'

"She looked at him as only mothers look.

The Sea-Serpent

'Each day these four years, I have laid fresh furs on your bed. Sleep now and rest, oh my Tenas Tyee,' she said."

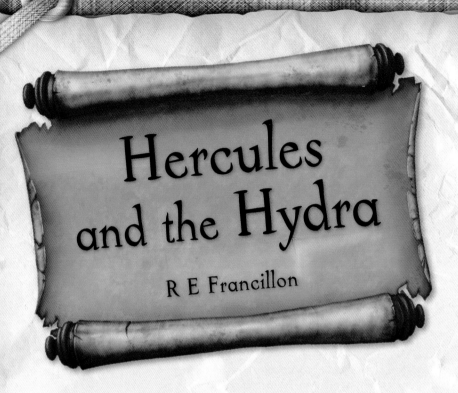

Hercules and the Hydra

R E Francillon

Hercules has been given the task of performing twelve labours by King Eurystheus. The second of these labours is to kill the terrible twelve-headed monster, the Hydra.

The Hydra was a huge water-snake, which lived in Lake Lerna, from where it used to go forth to find humans to eat. It had a hundred heads, and from each of its hundred mouths darted a forked tongue of flame, dripping with poison.

Hercules and the Hydra

Hercules set forth for Lake Lerna. But he did not go to work without making plans and taking all the precautions he could think of. He remembered the thickness and toughness of the Nemaean lion's skin, which he had just killed, so he had it made into a sort of cloak, which served him for armour better than brass or steel. He also made a young oak-tree into a regular club, which became his favourite weapon. And instead of going alone, he took with him his friend and cousin, Iolas, to act as his squire. You can always know Hercules in pictures and statues by his knotted club and his lion-skin.

It was easy enough to find the Hydra – only too easy. It had its nest in a foul swamp, the air of which its breath turned to poison. Giving Iolas his other weapons to

hold, Hercules attacked the
Hydra with his club alone,
trusting his lion-skin to
protect him from the
creature's fangs. With a
tremendous blow he
crushed one of the
Hydra's hundred heads,
leaving ninety-nine more
to destroy if he could hold
out so long.

That was bad enough
to think of – but, to his
dismay, out of the
crushed head sprang
two new living heads.
Then out of each of
these, when he beat

them to pieces, sprang two more, and so it was with every head the Hydra had. In truth, the more Hercules destroyed it, the stronger it grew – its hundred heads were rapidly becoming a thousand, and the thousand would become ten thousand, and so on, forever.

Just as Hercules realized the hopelessness of the labour, and was finding it work enough to ward off the innumerable fangs, a wretched crab crawled out of the ooze and seized him by the foot. He almost fainted with the sudden pain. It was too cruel, in the middle of such a battle as that, to feel himself suffer this extra pain.

However, he crushed the crab under his heel, and, stopping killing the heads, contented himself with defence, while he thought what could possibly be done.

'Those first hundred heads must all have come from one head,' thought he. 'They could not grow like that without a root. So if I could only destroy the root they would stop growing. This is my mistake – I am fighting only with what I see, instead of going to the root of things and attacking the evil there.'

So he called out to Iolas to heat a piece of iron red-hot and stand by when this was ready, and to scorch with it the place of every head that the club shattered. The plan worked wonderfully. Hercules crushed head after head, Iolas burned the stumps with the red-hot iron, and so root after root was burnt up and perished. At last they came to the root of all the heads, and when this was reached and burned, the monster sputtered and died, just when Hercules felt that, strong as he was, he could scarcely strike another blow.

Hercules cut open the Hydra and dipped his arrows in its poison, so that they should give deadly wounds. Then, wearily, he returned to Mycenae hoping for a little rest.

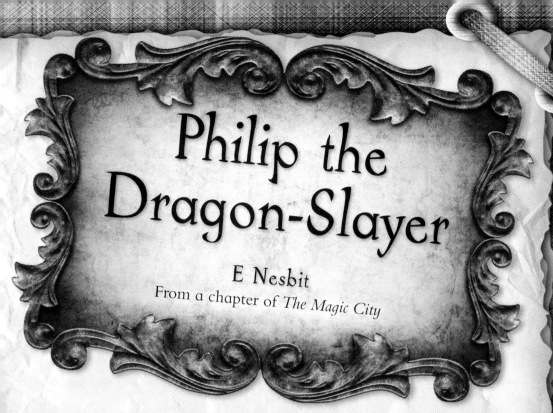

Philip the Dragon-Slayer

E Nesbit
From a chapter of *The Magic City*

Philip has found himself shrunken and trapped with his step-sister, Lucy, inside a city he has built out of his bricks and toys. The other toys have asked him to kill a dragon.

Philip was left alone. His first act was to go up to the top of the tower and look out to see if he could see the dragon. He looked east and north and south and west. Something was moving. Something long and jointed and green. It could be nothing but the dragon.

"Oh, crikey!" said Philip, "Whatever shall I do? Perhaps I'd better see what weapons there are."

So he ran down the stairs till he came to the vaults of the castle, and there he found everything a dragon-slayer could possibly need, even a little red book called *The Young Dragon-Catcher's Guide.*

The top of the tower seemed the safest place. It was there that he tried to read the book. The words were very long and most difficultly spelt. But he did manage to make out that all dragons sleep for one hour after sunset. Then he heard a loud rattling sound from the ruin, and he knew it was the dragon who was making that sound.

As he looked, he started, and then he said

in amazement, "That old thing!"

Then he looked again, and this is what he saw. An enormous green dragon, very long and fierce-looking, that rattled as it moved, rubbing itself against the fallen pillars. And the reason Philip laughed was that he knew that dragon very well indeed. It was the clockwork lizard that had been given to him the Christmas before last.

Philip remembered that he had put it into one of the cities he had built. Only now, of course, it had grown big and had come alive like all the other live things he had put in his cities. But he saw that it was still a clockwork creature – its key was sticking out of its side. It was rubbing itself against the pillars so as to turn the key and wind itself up, but this was not half done when the sun set. The dragon instantly lay down and went to sleep.

"Well," said the Dragon-Slayer, "now I've got to think."

He did think, harder than he had ever done before. And when he had finished thinking he went down into the vault and got a long rope. Then he stood still a moment, wondering if he really were brave enough. He went out in the dusk towards the dragon.

He knew it would sleep for an hour. There it lay – about ten or twelve yards of solid dark dragon-flesh. Its metal claws gleamed in the last of the daylight. Its great mouth was open and its breathing, as it slept, was like the sound of the sea on a rough night.

He walked along close to the
dragon till he came to the middle
part where the key was sticking.
Philip fastened one end of his rope
very securely to the key while the

dragon lay quite still. Then the Dragon-Slayer fastened the other end of the rope to the main wall of the ruin, which was very strong and firm.

You see the idea? It was really rather a clever one. When the dragon woke it would find that it was held prisoner by the rope. It would be furious and try to get free. And in its struggles it would be certain to get free, but this it could only do by detaching itself from its key. Once the key was out, the dragon would be unable to wind itself up any more and would be as good as dead. It was, as you see, an excellent plan, as far as it went.

Then the dragon woke up. Philip could see the great creature stretching itself and shaking its vast head as a dog does when it comes out of the water.

And now the dragon saw the Princess who had been placed at a convenient spot about half-way between the ruins and Philip's tower.

It threw up its snout and uttered a devastating howl, and Philip felt with a thrill of horror that, clockwork or no clockwork, the brute was alive and desperately dangerous.

It had perceived that it was bound. With great heavings and throes, with snortings and bellowings, with scratchings and tearings of its great claws and lashings of its terrible tail, it fought to be free.

Then what Philip had known would happen, did happen. With an echoing grinding rusty sound, the key was drawn

from the keyhole and left still fast to its rope
like an anchor to a cable.

Then something happened that Philip
had not foreseen. He had forgotten that,
before it fell asleep, the dragon had partly
wound itself up. Its struggles had not used
up all the winding. With a yell of fury it set
off across the plain, wriggling its green
rattling length towards the Princess!

Now there was no time to think
whether one was afraid or
not. Philip went down
those tower stairs
more quickly than
he had ever gone
down stairs in his life.

He put his sword over
his shoulder and ran. Like

the dragon, he
made straight for the
Princess. And now it
was a race between him
and the dragon. Philip ran
and ran. His heart thumped,
his feet had that leaden feeling
that comes in nightmares. Keep
on, keep on, faster, faster, you
mustn't stop.

How he did it, Philip never knew. But
with a last spurt he reached the pillar where
the Princess stood bound. The dragon was

twenty yards away, coming on and on.
Philip stood quite still, recovering his
breath. And more and more slowly, but
with no sign of stopping, the dragon
came on. Behind him, where the pillar
was, Philip heard the Princess crying
very softly.

Then the dragon was
quite near. Philip took
three steps

Philip the Dragon-Slayer

forward, took aim with his sword, shut his eyes and hit as hard as he could. Then something hard and heavy knocked him over, and for a time he knew no more.

When he came to himself again, Mr Noah was patting him on the back, all the people were shouting like mad, and beside him lay the dragon, lifeless and still.

"Oh!" said Philip, "did I really do it?"

"You did indeed," said Mr Noah, "however you may succeed with the other deeds, you are definitely the hero of this one. And now, if you feel well enough, prepare to receive the reward."

"Oh!" said Philip, brightening, "I didn't know there was to be a reward."

"Only the usual one," said Mr Noah. "The Princess, you know."

Philip became aware that a figure in a white veil was standing quite near him, and round its feet lay lengths of cut rope.

"The Princess is yours," said Mr Noah.

"But I don't want her," said Philip, adding by an afterthought, "thank you."

"That's not my affair," said Mr Noah. "She is waiting for you to take her by the hand and raise her veil."

"Must I?" said Philip miserably. "Well, here goes."

He took a small cold hand in one of his and with the other lifted, very gingerly, a corner of the veil. The other hand of the

Philip the Dragon-Slayer

Princess drew back the veil, and the Dragon-Slayer and the Princess were face to face.

"Why!" cried Philip "it's Lucy!"

Raiko Slays the Demon

William Elliot Griffis

In the hill country of Japan grew up a brave young warrior and clever archer. On account of his skill in the use of the bow, he was called to guard the Emperor's palace. At that time, the Emperor could not sleep at night because his rest was disturbed by a frightful beast, which scared away even the soldiers in armour who stood on guard.

Raiko Slays the Demon

This dreadful beast had the wings of a bird, the body and claws of a tiger, the head of a monkey, a serpent's tail, and the crackling scales of a dragon. Every night

45

it landed upon the roof of the palace, and howled and scratched so dreadfully that the poor Emperor grew weak and thin. None of the guards dared to face it in hand-to-hand combat, and none had skill enough to hit it with an arrow in the dark, though several of them tried.

The young archer decided to fight the beast come what might. So he strung his bow carefully, sharpened his steel-headed arrows, stored his quiver, and stood guard alone, except for his favourite servant.

It chanced to be a stormy night. The lightning was very bright, and the thunder-demon was beating all his drums. The wind swirled around frightfully, as though the wind-imp were emptying all his bags. Towards midnight, the hawk-eye of the

Raiko Slays the Demon

archer saw, during a flash of lightning, the awful beast sitting at the tip of the ridge-pole, on the north-east end of the roof. He told his servant to have a torch of straw and twigs ready to light at a moment's notice. Then he fitted the notch of his best arrow into the silk cord of his bow.

Keeping his eyes strained, he soon saw the glare of one eye, now two eyes. The beast, with a swaying head, crept along the great roof to the place on the eaves directly over the Emperor's sleeping room, and there it stopped.

This was the archer's opportunity. Aiming about a foot to the right of where he saw the eye glare, he drew his yard-length arrow shaft clear back to his shoulder, and let fly. A dull thud, a frightful howl, a heavy

SCALES AND TAILS

bump on the ground, and the writhing of some creature among the pebbles told in a few seconds' time that the arrow had struck flesh. The next instant the servant rushed out with the blazing torch and joined in the battle with his knife. A short but fierce three-cornered fight ensued, but the warrior's sharp sword soon finished the monster by cutting his throat. Then they skinned it, and the next morning the hide was shown to His Majesty.

All congratulated the brave archer on his valour and marksmanship. Many young men, sons of nobles and warriors, begged to become his pupils in archery. The Emperor ordered a noble to present him with a famous sword named 'The King of Wild

SCALES AND TAILS

Boars' and a lovely maid of honour begged to be his wife. He was promoted to captain of the guard, and given a high-sounding title. But he was also called Raiko, and by this name he is best known to all the boys and girls in Great Japan, who tell many tales of his skill and bravery.

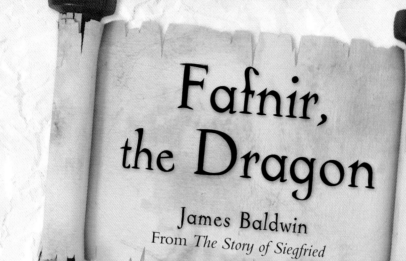

Fafnir, the Dragon

James Baldwin
From *The Story of Siegfried*

*Siegfried is a great warrior. He always travels with
Greyfell, a white horse with a gleaming mane. Siegfried
and Regin are on their way to try and kill Fafnir.*

Early in the morning, Siegfried
mounted Greyfell, and rode out
towards the desert land that lay beyond the
forest and the barren mountain range. For
seven days they wended their way through
the thick forest, sleeping at night on the

bare ground beneath the trees, while the wolves and other wild beasts of the forest filled the air with their hideous howlings. But no evil creature dared come near them, for fear of the shining beams of light which fell from Greyfell's gleaming mane.

On the eighth day they came to the open country and to the hills, where the land was covered with black boulders. No living thing was seen there, not even an insect nor a blade of grass, and the silence of the grave was over all. The earth was dry and the sun hung above them like a painted shield in a blue-black sky, and there was neither shade nor water anywhere. But Siegfried rode onwards. Towards the evening of the next day they came to a dark mountain wall that stretched far out on either side, and rose high above them.

Slowly and painfully, they climbed the steep cliff, sometimes following a narrow path that wound along the edge of a precipice, sometimes leaping from rock to rock or over some deep gorge, and sometimes picking their way among the crags and cliffs. The sun at last went down, and one by one the stars came out. The moon was rising, round and red, when Siegfried stood by Regin's side and gazed from the mountain-top down upon the Glittering Heath that lay beyond.

And a strange, weird scene it was that met his eyes. At the foot of the mountain was a river, white and cold and still. Beyond it was a smooth and barren plain, lying silent and lonely in the pale moonlight. As

SCALES AND TAILS

Fafnir, the Dragon

Siegfried gazed upon the scene, he saw the dim outline of some hideous monster moving, and seeming all the more terrible in the uncertain light.

"It is he!" whispered Regin in fear, "It is Fafnir, the Dragon! Should we not go back? Or will you dare to go forward and meet the dragon?"

"None but cowards give up," answered Siegfried. "Go back if you are afraid, but you must go alone. You have brought me to meet the dragon of the heath. Before the setting of another sun, the deed which you have urged me to do will be done."

Then he dashed down the eastern slope of the mountain, leaving Greyfell and the trembling Regin behind him. Soon he stood on the banks of the white river, which lay between the mountain and the heath, but the stream was deep and the channel was very wide. He paused a moment, wondering how he should cross. While he stood, a boat came silently out of the mists and drew near. The boatman stood up and called to him, "What man are you who dares come into this land of loneliness and fear?"

"I am Siegfried," answered the lad, "and I have come to slay Fafnir, the Dragon."

"Sit in my boat," said the boatman, "and I will carry you across the river."

Siegfried stepped in and sat by the boatman's side, and the little vessel turned and moved towards the farther shore.

"In what way will you fight the dragon?" asked the boatman.

Fafnir, the Dragon

"With my trusty sword Balmung," answered Siegfried.

"But he breathes deathly poisons, and his eyes dart forth lightning, and no man can withstand his strength," said the boatman.

"I will find some way by which to overcome him."

"Then be wise, and listen to me," said the boatman. "As you go up from the river you will find a road, worn deep and smooth, starting from the water's edge and winding over the moor. It is the trail of Fafnir, down which he comes at dawn of every day to drink at the river. Dig a pit in this road and hide yourself within it. In the morning, when Fafnir passes over it, let him feel the edge of Balmung."

As the man ceased speaking, the boat

touched the shore, and Siegfried leapt out. He looked back to thank his unknown friend, but neither boat nor boatman was to be seen. Then the lad remembered that the strange boatman had worn a blue hood with golden stars, and that his one eye glistened and sparkled with a light that was more than human. Siegfried knew that he had talked with Odin.

Then, with a braver heart than before, he went forward along the river bank, until he came to Fafnir's trail – a deep, wide furrow in the earth, beginning at the river's bank and winding far away over the heath. The bottom of the trail was soft and slimy, and its sides had been worn smooth by Fafnir's travel through it.

In this road, Siegfried, with his trusty

sword Balmung, scooped out a deep and narrow pit. When the grey dawn began to appear in the east, he hid himself within this pit and waited for the coming of Fafnir.

He had not long to wait, for no sooner had the sky begun to redden in the light of the coming sun than the dragon was heard. Siegfried peeped from his hiding place, and saw him coming far down the road. With bloodshot eyes, gaping mouth and flaming nostrils, the hideous creature came rushing onwards. His sharp, curved claws dug deep into the soft earth, and his bat–like wings half trailed on the ground, half flapped in the air.

It was a terrible moment for Siegfried, but still he was not afraid. He crouched low down in his hiding place, and the bare blade of the trusty Balmung glittered in the morning light.

On came the hastening feet, and the red gleam from the monster's flaming nostrils lit up the pit where Siegfried lay. Then a black, inky mass rolled above him. Now was his chance. The bright edge of Balmung struck the heart of Fafnir as he passed.

The monster stopped short, while but half of his long body had glided over the pit, for sudden death had overtaken him. His horrid head fell lifeless upon the ground. His cold wings flapped once, and then lay, quivering and helpless, spread out on either side. Streams of thick, black blood flowed from his heart, through the wound beneath, and filled the trench in which Siegfried was hidden. It ran like a mountain torrent down

the road towards the river. Siegfried was
covered from head to foot with the slimy
liquid, and, had he not quickly leapt from
his hiding place, he would have been
drowned in the swift-rushing stream.

The bright sun rose in the east, covering
the mountain tops, and fell upon the still
waters of the river, lighting up the treeless
plains around. The sound of singing birds
and rippling waters – such as had not
broken the silence of the Glittering Heath
for ages – came to Siegfried's ears. The
dragon was dead, and Nature had
awakened from her sleep of dread. The
shining Greyfell stood by his side.

Siegfried turned his back on the fearful
scene, and rode away. So swiftly did
Greyfell carry him over the desert land and

Fafnir, the Dragon

the mountain waste, that, when night came, they stood on the shore of the great North Sea and the white waves broke at their feet.

St George and the Dragon

Flora Annie Steel

S t George, the bold knight, rode on his horse, Bayard, seeking to do good and fight evil. This is the story of an adventure he had in the land of Egypt.

It began when, on his travels, St George came to a chapel, where he begged to stay for the night. The monk who lived there said, "Sir Knight of Merrie England – for I see England's cross on your shield – you have come here in an evil time. We have a terrible dragon that rages up and down the country by day and by night. If he is not given an innocent maiden to devour each day, he sends a deadly plague among the people. This has not stopped for twenty and four years, so that there is only one maiden left – the beautiful Sâbia, daughter to the King. Tomorrow she will die, unless some brave knight will slay the monster. To anyone who can perform this deed, the King offers his crown and the hand of his daughter in marriage."

"I don't care about crowns," said St George boldly, "but the beautiful maiden shall not die. I will slay the monster."

So, rising at dawn of day, he buckled on his armour, laced his helmet, and with his

sword Ascalon in his
hand, he mounted
Bayard and rode into the
Valley of the Dragon.
Now on the way he met a
procession of old women weeping
and wailing, and in the middle was
the most beautiful woman he had ever
seen. St George got off his horse and bowed
low before the lady, telling her to return to
her father's palace, since he was about to
kill the dreaded dragon. The beautiful Sâbia
thanked him with smiles and tears, and he
rode on to his adventure.

Now, no sooner did the dragon catch
sight of the brave Knight than its leathery
throat sent out a sound more terrible than
thunder, and coming out from its hideous

St George and the Dragon

den, it spread its burning wings and prepared to attack. Its size and appearance might well have made the bravest man tremble. It was a full forty feet from shoulder to tail, its body was covered with green scales, its belly was as gold, and through its flaming wings the blood ran thick and red.

Its attack was so fierce, the Knight was nearly knocked to the ground. But recovering himself, St George gave the dragon a thrust with his spear. The furious monster then struck him so violently with its tail that both horse and rider were thrown over.

SCALES AND TAILS

Now, by great good chance, St George was flung under the shade of a flowering orange tree, whose scent has such power that no poisonous beast dare come within its branches. So lying under the tree he had time to recover.

When he had got his strength back, he rose and struck the burning dragon on his belly with his trusty sword Ascalon. There spouted out poison of such strength that it ate away the armour of the bold Knight, which dropped off him.

It might have gone very badly with St George of Merrie England if it wasn't for the orange tree, which once again gave him

St George and the Dragon

shelter under its branches.
Then, with a bold heart, he
came forward again, and
struck the fiery dragon
under one of its flaming
wings so that the weapon
pierced its heart. All the
grass around turned crimson
with the blood that flowed
from the dying monster.

So St George of England
cut off the dreadful head and, hanging it on
a shaft of his spear that had broken, he
mounted his steed Bayard, and rode on to
the palace of the King.

Now the King's name was Ptolemy, and
when he saw that the dreaded dragon was
indeed killed, he gave orders for the city to

be decorated. He sent a golden chariot with wheels of ebony and cushions of silk to bring St George to the palace. The King also commanded a hundred noblemen dressed in crimson velvet and mounted on milk-white horses to escort him there, while musicians walked in front of him, filling the air with sweetest sounds.

The beautiful Sâbia herself washed and bandaged the weary Knight's wounds. Then, after he had been magnificently feasted, he lay down to rest, while the beautiful Sâbia from her balcony lulled him to sleep with her golden lute.

The Laidly Worm

Flora Annie Steel

'Laidly Worm' is what people in the north of England used to say to mean a hideous serpent.

In Bamborough Castle there once lived a king who had two children, a son named Childe Wynde and a daughter who was called May Margret. Their mother was dead, and the King mourned her long and faithfully. But after his son Childe Wynde went to seek his fortune, the King, hunting in the forest, came across a lady of such great beauty that he fell in love with her at once and determined to marry her.

Now Princess May Margret said nothing, though she stood long on the castle walls looking out across the sea wishing for her dear brother's return, for, you see, they had mothered each other.

Still no news came of Childe Wynde, so on the day when the old King was to bring the new Queen home, May Margret stood at the Castle gate ready to hand over the keys to her step-mother.

As the bridal procession approached with all the lords in attendance, she looked so fair and so sweet, that the lords whispered to one another of her beauty saying she was the fairest lady in all the land. The new

The Laidly Worm

Queen overheard this and she stamped her foot, and her face flushed with anger.

That same night the new Queen, who was also a witch, left her royal bed and, returning to the lonely cave where she did her magic, cast Princess May Margret under a spell with charms three times three, and passes nine times nine. And this was her spell:

"*I turn you to a Laidly Worm,*
And such shall ye ever be
Until Childe Wynde, the King's dear son,
Comes home across the sea.

Until the world comes to an end
Unspelled you'll never be,
Unless Childe Wynde of his own free will
Shall give you kisses three!"

Scales and Tails

So it came to pass that Princess May Margret went to her bed a maiden, full of grace, and rose next morning a Laidly Worm. When her maids came to dress her they found coiled up in her bed an awesome dragon, which uncoiled itself and came toward them. When they ran away terrified, the Laidly Worm crawled and

The Laidly Worm

crept, and crept and crawled down to the sea. And there it curled itself round a stone and lay basking in the sun.

Then for seven miles east and seven miles west and seven miles north and south, the whole countryside knew the hunger of the Laidly Worm. It drove the awesome beast to leave its resting place at night and devour everything it came across.

At last a wise warlock told the people that if they wished to be rid of these horrors, they must take the milk of seven white cows every morning and every evening for the Laidly Worm to drink. This they did, and after that the Laidly Worm troubled the countryside no longer, but lay looking out to sea with its terrible snout in the air.

But the word of its doings had gone east
and had gone west. It had even gone over
the sea and had come to Childe Wynde's
ears. So he called his men-at-arms together
and said, "We must sail to Bamborough and
kill this Laidly Worm."

Then they built a ship without delay,
laying the keel with wood from the rowan
tree. They made masts of rowan wood also,
and set forth.

One morning the wicked Queen, looking
from the castle, saw the gallant ship in
Bamborough Bay, and she sent out all her
witch-wives and her imps to raise a storm
and sink the ship. But they came back
unable to hurt it, for it was built of rowan
wood, and witches have no power over that.

Then the Witch Queen laid spells upon

The Laidly Worm

the Laidly Worm to attack the ship.

Now the Laidly Worm had no choice but to obey. So three times three did Childe Wynde attempt to land, and three times three the Laidly Worm kept the good ship from the shore, but he was not to be beaten. Childe Wynde rounded the next point to Budley sands, and there, jumping into the water, he got safely to land, and drawing his sword, rushed up to fight the awesome Worm. But as he raised his sword to strike he heard a voice, soft as the western wind, telling him to put up his sword and give three kisses to the Worm.

The voice seemed to him like the voice of his dear sister, May Margret. So Childe Wynde, remembering how he had loved his sister, put his arms round the Laidly Worm and kissed it once. And he kissed the loathly thing twice. And he kissed it yet a third time as he stood with the wet sand at his feet.

Then with a hiss and a roar, the Laidly Worm sank to the sand, and in his arms was May Margret!

He wrapped her in his cloak, for she trembled in the cold sea air, and carried her to Bamborough Castle. The wicked Queen, knowing her hour was come, stood, deserted by her imps and witch-wives, on the stairs, twisting her hands.

Then Childe Wynde, looking at her, cried, "Woe to you, wicked Queen! The curse you put on my sister shall come now upon you."

And as he spoke the wicked Queen began to shrivel, and she shrivelled and shrivelled to a wrinkled toad that hopped down the castle steps and disappeared.

To this day a loathsome toad is sometimes seen haunting Bamborough Castle, and that Laidly Toad is the wicked Witch Queen! But Childe Wynde and Princess May Margret both lived happily ever after.

The Mighty Monster Afang

William Elliot Griffis

*This story uses the old belief that a young
girl could tame a monster by singing to it.*

After the Welsh had come up from
Cornwall into their new land, they
began to cut down the trees to build towns,
and to have fields and gardens.

While they were draining the swamps
and bogs, they drove out the monsters that
had made their lairs in these wet places.

The Mighty Monster Afang

These terrible creatures liked to poison people with their bad breath, and even ate up little boys and girls when they strayed away from home.

Now there was a great monster named the Afang that lived in a big bog, hidden among the high hills and inside of a dark, rough forest.

This ugly creature had an iron-clad back, and a long tail that could wrap itself around a mountain. It had four front legs, with big knees that were bent up like a grasshopper's, but were covered with scales like armour. These were as hard as steel, and bulged out at the thighs. Along its back, was a ridge of horns like spines, and higher than an alligator's. Against such a tough hide, when the hunters shot their darts and hurled their javelins, these weapons fell down to the ground like harmless pins.

On this great monster's head were big ears, halfway between those of a donkey and an elephant. Its eyes were round and as green as leeks, while they were as big as pumpkins.

But after its dinner, when the creature had swallowed down a man, or two calves, or four sheep, or a cow, or three goats, its body swelled up like a big balloon. Then it usually lay along the ground or in the soft mud, and felt very stupid and sleepy

The Mighty Monster Afang

for a long while.

All around its lair lay loads of bones of creatures, girls, women, men, boys, cows, and occasionally a donkey. Someone may ask, why did not some brave man shoot the monster with a poisoned arrow, or drive a spear into him under the arms where the flesh was tender, or cut off his head with a sharp sword?

The trouble was just here. There were plenty of brave fellows ready to fight the monster, but nothing made of iron could pierce that hide of his. It was like armour.

Nothing would do, but to go up into his lair and drag him out.

But what man or company of men was strong enough to do this, when a dozen giants in a gang, with thick ropes, could hardly tackle the job?

However, one brave girl volunteered to bind the monster in his lair. She said, "I'm not afraid." Her sweetheart was named Gadern, and he was a young and strong hunter. He talked over the matter with her and they planned it together.

Gadern went all over the country, summoning the farmers to bring their ox teams and log chains. Then he set the blacksmiths to work, forging new and especially heavy chains, made of the best native iron from the mines, for which

The Mighty Monster Afang

Wales is still famous.

Meanwhile, the lovely maiden dressed herself in her prettiest clothes, arranged her hair in the most enticing way, and hung a white blossom on each side, over her ears, with one flower also at her neck.

When she had perfumed her garments, she went up the lake where the big bog and the waters were and where the monster hid himself.

While the maiden was still quite a distance away, the terrible Afang, scenting his visitor from afar, came rushing out of his lair. When very near, he reared his head high in the air, expecting to pounce on her with his iron-clad claws.

The girl was not at all afraid, but smoothed the monster's back and tickled its neck until the Afang's throat actually gurgled with a laugh. When he did this, the people down in the valley thought it was thunder, though the sky was clear and blue.

The maiden tickled his chin, and soon she had gently lulled him to sleep, by singing a cradle song. This she did so softly and sweetly, that in a few minutes, with its head in her lap, the monster was sound asleep and even began to snore.

Then, quietly, from their hiding places in the bushes, Gadern and his men crawled out. When near the dreaded Afang, they stood up and sneaked forward very softly on tiptoe. They had wrapped the links of the chain in grass and leaves, so that no clanking was heard. Slowly but surely they passed the chain over its body in the middle, besides tying it tightly between its fore and hind legs.

All this time, the monster slept on, for the girl kept on crooning her melody.

When the forty oxen were all harnessed together, the drivers cracked all their whips at the same time, so that it sounded like a

clap of thunder, and the whole team began
to pull together.

The sudden jerk made the monster angry,
and its bellowing was terrible. It rolled
round and round, and dug its four sets of
toes, each with three claws, into the ground.
It tried hard to crawl into its lair or slip into
the lake.

Finding that neither was possible, the
Afang looked about for some big tree to
wrap its tail around. But all his writhings
and plungings were of no use.

In a great hole in the ground big enough
to be a pond, they dumped the Afang, and
soon a little lake was formed. This strange
bit of water is called 'The Lake of the Green
Well'. It is considered dangerous for man or
beast to go too near it. Birds do not like to

The Mighty Monster Afang

fly over the surface, and when sheep tumble in, they sink to the bottom at once.

As for Gadern and his brave and lovely sweetheart, they were married and lived long and happily. All farmers honour his memory and bless the name of the lovely girl that sang the monster to sleep.

The Quarrelsome Dragons

L Frank Baum

From *The Tin Man of Oz*

Woot, a Green Monkey, and his friends have stolen a magic apron that can make anything open when you say the word 'Open'. The earth has opened underneath Woot.

The Green Monkey sank gently into the earth for a little way and then tumbled swiftly through space, landing on a rocky floor with a thump that astonished him. Then he sat up, found that no bones were broken, and gazed around him.

The Quarrelsome Dragons

He seemed to be in a big underground cave, which was dimly lit by dozens of big round discs that looked like moons. They were not moons, however, as Woot discovered when he had examined the place more carefully. They were eyes. The eyes were in the heads of enormous beasts whose bodies trailed far behind them.

Each beast was bigger than an elephant, and three times as long, and there were a dozen or more of the creatures scattered here and there about the cavern. On their bodies were big scales, as round as pie-plates, which were beautifully tinted in shades of green, purple and orange. On the ends of their long tails were clusters of bright jewels.

Woot saw that the creatures had wide

mouths and rows of terrible
teeth. From tales he had heard
of such beings, he knew they
were the great Dragons that had
been driven from the surface of
the earth, and were only allowed to
come out once in a hundred years to
search for food.

The Green Monkey sat upon the floor
where he had fallen, staring around, and
the owners of the big
eyes returned his look,

92

silently. Finally one of the Dragons asked, in a deep, grave voice, "What was that?"

And the greatest Dragon of all, who was just in front of the Green Monkey, answered in a still deeper voice, "It is some foolish animal from Outside."

"Is it good to eat?" inquired a smaller Dragon beside the great one. "I'm hungry."

"Hungry!" exclaimed all the Dragons together, and then the great one said, "Tut-tut, my son! You've no reason to be hungry at this time."

"Why not?" asked the little Dragon. "I haven't eaten anything in eleven years."

"Eleven years is absolutely nothing," remarked another of the Dragons, sleepily opening and closing his eyes, "I haven't feasted for eighty-seven years. Children who eat between meals should be broken of the habit."

"All I had, eleven years ago, was a rhinoceros, and that's not a full meal at all," grumbled the young one. "And before that I had waited sixty-two years to be fed, so it's no wonder I'm hungry."

"How old are you now?" asked Woot, forgetting his own danger in his interest in the conversation.

"Why, I'm – I'm – How old am I, Father?" asked the little Dragon.

"Goodness gracious! What a child to ask questions. Don't you know that thinking is very bad for Dragons?" said the big Dragon, impatiently.

"How old am I, Father?" persisted the small Dragon.

"About six hundred and thirty, I believe. Ask your mother."

"No, don't!" said an old Dragon in the background. "Haven't I enough worries, what with being wakened in the middle of a nap, without having to keep track of my children's ages?"

"You've been fast asleep for over sixty years, Mother," said the child Dragon. "How long a nap do you want?"

"I should have slept forty years longer. And this strange little green beast should be punished for falling into our cavern and disturbing us."

"I didn't know you were here, and I didn't know I was going to fall in," explained Woot.

"Nevertheless, here you are," said the

great Dragon, "and you have carelessly woken our entire tribe, so it stands to reason you must be punished."

"In what way?" inquired the Green Monkey, trembling a little.

"Give me time and I'll think of a way. You're in no hurry, are you?" asked the great Dragon.

"No, indeed," cried Woot. "Take your time. I'd much rather you'd all go to sleep again, and punish me when you wake up in a hundred years or so."

"Please let me eat him!" exclaimed the littlest Dragon.

"He is too small," said the father Dragon. "To eat this one Green Monkey would only make you hungry for more, and there are no more."

SCALES AND TAILS

"Stop this chatter and let me get to sleep," said another Dragon, yawning in a fearful manner, for when he opened his mouth a sheet of flame leapt out from it and made Woot jump back.

In his jump he bumped against the nose

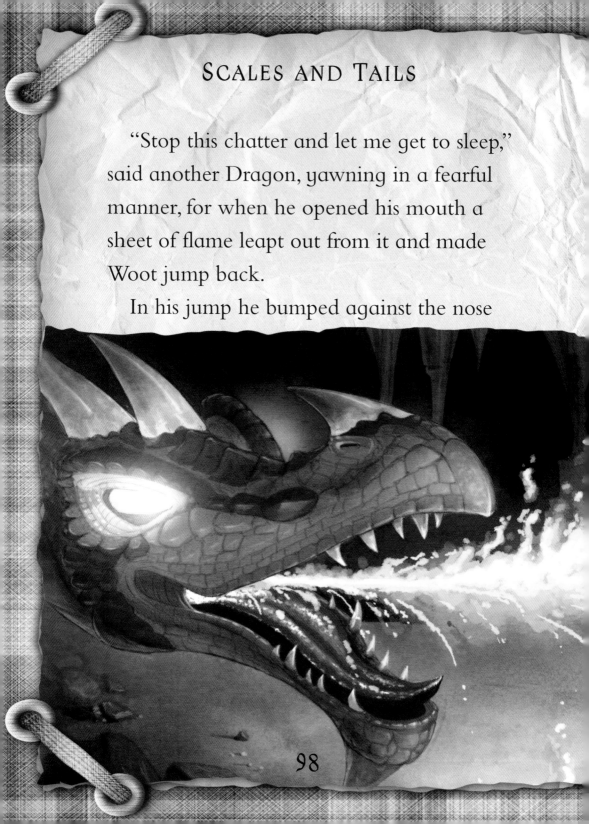

The Quarrelsome Dragons

of a Dragon behind him, which opened its mouth to growl and shot another sheet of flame at him. The flame was bright, but not very hot, yet Woot screamed with terror and sprang forward with a great bound. This time he landed on the paw of the great

Chief Dragon, who angrily raised his other front paw and struck the Green Monkey a fierce blow. Woot went sailing through the air and fell sprawling upon the rocky floor.

All the great beasts were now thoroughly awakened, and they blamed the monkey for disturbing their quiet. The littlest Dragon darted after Woot and the others followed, flashing from their eyes and mouths flames which lighted up the entire cavern. Woot almost gave up at that moment, but he scrambled to his feet and dashed away to the farthest end of the cave, the Dragons following more slowly because they were too clumsy to move fast. Perhaps they thought there was no need to hurry as the monkey could not escape from the cave.

But at the end of the place, the cavern

The Quarrelsome Dragons

floor was heaped with tumbled rocks, so Woot climbed from rock to rock until he found himself crouched against the cavern roof. There he waited, for he could go no farther, while on over the tumbled rocks slowly crept the Dragons – the littlest one coming first because he was hungry as well as angry.

The beasts had almost reached him when Woot, remembering his lace apron, recovered his wits and shouted, "Open!" At the cry a hole appeared in the roof of the cavern just above his head, and through it the sunlight streamed down upon the Green Monkey.

The Dragons paused, astonished at the magic and blinking at the sunlight, and this gave Woot time to climb through the opening. As soon as he reached the surface of the earth the hole closed again, and the Green Monkey realized with a thrill of joy that he had seen the last of the dangerous Dragon family.

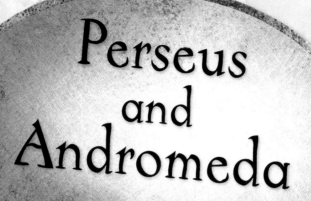

Perseus and Andromeda

R E Francillon

*The great Greek hero Perseus is travelling through
the lands around the Mediterranean Sea. An oracle was
a priest or priestess who foretold the future and gave
advice to people based on their prophecies.*

Perseus continued his journey, travelling on and on until he reached the coast of Ethiopia, and entered a great city on the seashore.

But though the place seemed great and

rich, the whole air was full of sadness and gloom. The people went about silent and sighing, and had no attention to spare for a stranger. When Perseus reached the King's palace the signs of sadness were deeper still.

"What is the matter?" asked Perseus at last, seizing a passing servant by the arm. "Is it the death of the King?"

"Ah, if it were only that!" said the man. "But no, King Cepheus is alive and well. Alas, and woe is me!" And so once more he fell to wailing, and passed on.

Over and over again Perseus tried to get an answer, but heard nothing but tears and groans. And so he went on till he reached a chamber where sat the King himself in the midst of his court.

"I see you are a stranger," said King

Perseus and Andromeda

Cepheus. "Pardon us if we have seemed unfriendly and unlike the Ethiopians, the friends of the gods. It is not our way. But," he continued, the tears flowing as he spoke, "if you knew, you would understand."

"Let me know," said Perseus gently, for he was filled with pity for the King's tears.

"My daughter, Princess Andromeda," answered the King, "is condemned to a horrible death. I do not know whether she is yet alive."

"How can a king's daughter be condemned to death against her father's will?" asked Perseus.

"No wonder it sounds strange," answered Cepheus, "but listen, Andromeda is my only child. For some reason the gods have permitted our land to be attacked by a monster that comes out of the sea and that spares neither man, woman, nor child. Not one of us is left without cause to mourn. Fearing that all my people would be destroyed, I asked the great oracle of Ammon in what way the monster could be stopped. Alas! The oracle said that the only thing that would work would be delivering up Andromeda herself to be eaten. What could I do? Could I let my people lose all their children for the sake of my own? There was only one thing for a king, who is the father of all his people, to do, and even now—" But he could say no more.

"Oracle or no oracle," said Perseus, "it shall not be while I am alive! Where is the princess now?"

"She was chained at sunrise to a rock on

the seashore, there to wait for the monster. But where she is now—"

Perseus did not wait for another word, but, leaving the palace, hurried along the shore, already half covered by the rising tide. At last he came to what made his heart beat and burn with pity and rage. Chained by her wrists to a pillar of rock was the most beautiful of all princesses, already nearly waist-high in the rising waves. What struck Perseus most was her look of quiet courage and noble pride – the look of one who was devoting herself to a cruel death for the country's sake, and in order that others might be saved.

The whole heart of Perseus went out to her. He vowed, if he could not save her, to share her death. But before he could reach

her side, a huge black wave parted, and out
came the monster – a creature like nothing
else of land or sea, with a swollen, shapeless
body, studded with hungry, cruel eyes, and
hundreds of long, slimy limbs, twisting and
crawling, each with a yawning mouth, from
which streamed fire and horrible fumes.

Andromeda turned pale as the creature
came on with a slowness more dreadful
than speed. Perseus could not wait.
Springing from the rock he threw himself,
like lightning, full upon the monster, and
then began such a struggle as had never
been seen before. The creature twined its
limbs around Perseus, and tried to crush
him. As soon as Perseus tore himself from
one, he was clutched by another.

Perseus felt his life passing from him. He

Perseus and Andromeda

put all the strength he had left into one last blow. It fell only on the monster's right shoulder. But that was the one place where it could be pierced. The coils relaxed, and Perseus, to his own amazement, saw the monster floating, a shapeless corpse, upon the waves.

Having released Andromeda, who had watched the struggle in dread for what had seemed the certain fate of her rescuer, he carried her back to her father's palace. I need not tell how the mourning turned into wonder and joy!

"What can I do to show my gratitude?" asked King Cepheus of Perseus. "Ask of me whatever you will, and it shall be yours, on the word of a king!"

"If she is willing, give me Andromeda to be my wife," said Perseus. "That is all I want in the world."

"Gladly," said Cepheus, but suddenly he looked serious. "I have promised you on the word of a king, which cannot be broken.

But I must warn you that you are not the first in the field. Andromeda has long been claimed in marriage by the powerful Prince Phineus, and he is not the man to lose what he wants without giving trouble."

"He never gave any trouble to the monster," said Perseus, thinking that Cepheus, though kind, was rather a weak and timid sort of king. So the marriage of Perseus and Andromeda was settled to the great joy of both, and all the nobles were invited to a great festival in honour of the wedding, and of the delivery of the land.

Boggarts, Trolls and Goblins

Farmer Griggs's Boggart

Howard Pyle

From *Pepper and Salt*

Did you ever hear of a boggart? No? Then I will tell you. A boggart is a small imp that lives in a man's house, unseen by anyone, doing a little good but a lot of harm. Even now you may find a boggart in some houses.

The snow lay all over the ground, like soft feathers. Icicles hung down from the roof of the farmhouse, and birds crouched

Farmer Griggs's Boggart

shivering in the bare, leafless hedgerows.

But inside the farmhouse all was warm and pleasant. Great logs snapped and crackled and roared in the wide chimney place, and Farmer Griggs sat warming his feet at the blaze.

Dame Griggs's spinning wheel went *humm-m-m*, *hum-m-m-m-m*, the cat purred in the warmth of the fire and the dog basked in the blaze.

But, *rap! tap! tap!* came a loud knock at the door.

So Farmer Griggs took his pipe out of his mouth and went to see who was there.

"Will you let me in out of the cold, Georgie Griggs?" piped a small voice. Farmer Griggs looked down and saw a little creature no taller than his knee standing in the snow on the doorstep. His face was brown and he looked up at the farmer with great eyes as bright as those of a toad. His feet were bare and he wore no clothes.

"Who are you, little man?" said Farmer Griggs.

"I'm a boggart, at your service, Georgie Griggs."

"No, no," said Farmer Griggs, "I'll give no room in my house to the likes of you." And he went to shut the door in the face of the little monster.

"But listen, Georgie Griggs," said the boggart, "I will work well for you."

Farmer Griggs's Boggart

Then Farmer Griggs did listen. "What will you do for me, then?" he asked.

"I'll tend your fires," said the little monster, "I'll bake your bread, I'll wash your dishes, I'll clean your pans, I'll scrub your floors, I'll brew your beer, I'll roast your meat, I'll boil your water, I'll stuff your sausages, I'll skim your milk, I'll make your butter, I'll knit your stockings, I'll mend your clothes, I'll patch your shoes – I'll be everywhere and do all of the work in your house!"

"I don't know," said Farmer Griggs, scratching his head doubtfully. "It's a bad thing letting mischief into the house! You're better outside, I'm quite sure."

"Shut the door, Georgie!" called out Dame Griggs.

Then Farmer Griggs shut the door, but the boggart was on the inside.

This is the way in which the boggart came into Farmer Griggs's house, and there he was to stay, for it is no easy matter getting rid of the likes of him once he is inside, I can tell you.

The boggart went over to the warm fire straight away. The cat spat at him in anger and jumped up on the dresser. But the boggart laid himself comfortably down among the warm ashes.

Now, imps, like this boggart, can only be seen as the frost is seen – when it is cold. So as the boggart grew warmer and warmer, he grew thinner and thinner! At last, when he had become thoroughly warmed through, Farmer Griggs and the dame could see him no more. But he was in the house and he stayed there.

For a time everything went smoothly. All of the housework was done as though by magic. The boggart did all that he had promised – he was everywhere and did all of the work in the house.

But after a time, the boggart began to play his pranks. He skimmed the children's milk so that they had nothing but watery stuff to pour over their porridge. He blew out the lights so that they were all in the dark, he made the fires burn cold, and he played one hundred and forty other impish tricks of the like.

However, the boggart did his housework
well, so Farmer Griggs put up with his evil
ways for as long as he could. At last the
time came when he could bear it no longer.
He knew you could not make a boggart
leave a house once it was in, so Farmer
Griggs decided they must go themselves.

So one fine bright day, they packed all of
their belongings into a great cart and set off
to find a new home.

As they came to the bottom of Shooter's
Hill, who should they meet but their good
neighbour, Jerry Jinks. "So, Georgie," he said,
"you're leaving the old house at last?"

"Hi, Jerry," said Georgie. "We were forced
to it, neighbour, for that boggart torments
us so that there was no rest."

Now on the cart was a tall, upright

Farmer Griggs's Boggart

churn. As soon as
Georgie Griggs had finished
talking, the lid of the churn began to
clipper-clapper, and who should speak out of
it but the boggart himself. "Ay, Jerry!" said
the boggart, "We're moving, man! Come
and see us soon!"

"What!" cried Georgie Griggs, "Are you

there, you black imp? Dang it! We'll all go back to the old house, then."

So back they went again – with boggart and all.

You see, if you warm an imp by your fire, he will soon turn the whole house topsy-turvy. One cannot get rid of a boggart by going from here to there, for it is sure to be in the cart with the household things.

But how did Georgie Griggs get rid of his boggart? I will tell you.

He went to see Father Grimes, the wise man who lived in a little house on the moor. "Father Grimes," said Farmer Griggs, "how should I get rid of my boggart?"

Then Father Grimes told him to take this and that, and to do thus and so with them, and see what followed. So Farmer

Farmer Griggs's Boggart

Griggs went and bought a pretty red coat, a neat pair of blue breeches and a nice velvet cap with a bell at the top of it. Then he went to Thomas the shoemaker's and got a fine pair of shoes. He laid them on a warm spot on the hearth where the boggart used to come to sleep at night. Then he and Dame Griggs hid and watched to see what would follow.

Presently in came the boggart, whisking here and dancing there, though neither the farmer nor the dame could see him any more than if he had been a puff of wind.

"Heigh-ho!" cried the boggart, "These are fine things for sure." He put them on and began dancing until he made the ashes on the hearth spin around. He went singing and dancing, and skipping and leaping, out of the house and away. As for Georgie Griggs and his dame, they never heard a squeak from him again.

And so it was that Farmer Griggs finally got rid of his boggart.

How an Old Man Lost His Wart

A traditional Japanese tale

Many many years ago in Japan there lived
a good old man who had a wart like a
tennis ball growing out of his right cheek.
He tried everything he could think of to get
rid of it, but it was all of no use.

One day the old man ran out of firewood,
so he took his axe and set out for the woods
up among the hills. When the day began to
draw to a close he started homewards.

The old man had not gone far on his way down the mountain when the sky clouded and rain began to fall heavily. He looked about for some shelter and at last he spied the hollow trunk of a tree. He crept in easily and sat down.

At last, the sky cleared as the sun started to set. The old man was about to step out from his hiding place when he saw hundreds of goblins coming towards the spot. Some of the goblins

How an Old Man Lost His Wart

were as large as giants, others had great big eyes, others had hugely long noses, and some had such big mouths that they opened from ear to ear. All of the goblins had horns growing on their foreheads. While the old man was sitting there in terror, he heard the sounds of music and then some of the goblins began to sing.

On peeping out, the old man saw that the Goblin Chief himself was actually sitting with his back against the hollow tree, and all the other goblins were sitting round him – some drinking and some dancing. It made the old man laugh to see their strange antics.

He was so interested and excited in watching all that the goblins were doing that he forgot himself, and stepped out of the tree and stood looking on.

The Goblin Chief was taking a big cup of wine and watching one of the goblins dancing. In a little while he said with a bored air, "Isn't there any one among you all who can dance better than this?"

The old man had been fond of dancing all his life and he knew that he could do much better than the goblin.

"Shall I go and dance before these goblins and let them see what a human being can do? It might be dangerous, for if I don't please them they may kill me!" said the old fellow to himself.

However, his fears were soon overcome by his love of dancing. In a few minutes he stepped out before the whole party of goblins and began to dance at once.

"How strange!" exclaimed the horned Goblin Chief. "I've never seen such a skilful dancer before!"

When the old man had finished his dance, the big goblin said, "Thank you very much for your amusing dance. You must come often. Your skill has given us much pleasure."

The old man thanked him (while all the time planning never to come near the spot ever again).

"Will you come again tomorrow old man?" asked the goblin.

"Certainly I will," answered the old man (but not meaning it).

"What is the best thing he can leave with us as a pledge that he will keep his word?" asked the Goblin Chief, looking round.

Then one of the goblin's attendants, kneeling behind the chief, said, "The token he leaves with us must be the most important thing in his possession. I see the old man has a wart on his right cheek. I believe humans consider such a wart very lucky. Let my lord take the lump from the old man's right cheek and he will surely come tomorrow, if only to get that back."

"You are very clever," said the Goblin Chief. Then he stretched out a hairy arm

and claw-like hand, and took the great
lump from the old man's right cheek.
Strange to say, it came off as easily as a ripe

plum from a tree, and then the merry troop
of goblins suddenly vanished.

Then the old man realized how late it
was and began to hurry home. He patted

his right cheek all the time, as if to make
sure of his good luck in having lost his wart.
He was so happy that he found it
impossible to walk quietly – he ran and
danced the whole way home.

The old man found his wife very worried,
wondering what had happened to make
him so late. He soon told her all that had
passed. She was as happy as her husband
when he showed her that the ugly lump
had disappeared from his face.

Now, next door to this good old couple
there lived a wicked and disagreeable old
man. He also had a wart on his left cheek
and had tried all manner of things to get
rid of it, but all in vain.

He heard at once of his neighbour's good
luck in losing the lump on his face, so he

called that very evening and asked his friend to tell him all about it. The good old man told him what had happened, and the wicked old man decided to see if he could have the same luck.

He started out the very next afternoon, and after hunting about for some time, came to the hollow tree trunk his friend had described. Here, he hid himself and waited for the twilight.

Just as he had been told, the band of goblins came at that hour and held a feast with dancing and singing. When this had gone on for some time the chief of the goblins looked around and said, "It is now time for the old man to come as he promised us. Why doesn't he come?"

When the wicked old man heard these

words he ran out of his hiding place in the tree and said, "Here I am!"

"Ah, you are the old man of yesterday," said the Goblin Chief, who could not tell humans apart. "Thank you for coming. You must dance for us."

The old man now stood up, opened his fan and began to dance. But he had never learned to dance and he thought that anything would please the goblins, so he just hopped about, waving his arms and stamping his feet.

The goblins said among themselves, "How badly he dances today!"

Then the Goblin Chief said to the old man, "Your performance today is quite different from the dance of yesterday. We don't wish to see any more of such dancing.

How an Old Man Lost His Wart

We will give you back the pledge you left with us. You must go away at once."

With these words he took out the wart that he had taken from the face of the old man who had danced so well the day before, and threw it at the right cheek of the old man who stood before him.

The lump immediately attached itself to his cheek as firmly as if it had grown there always, and all attempts to pull it off were useless. The wicked old man put one hand and then the other to each side of his face to make sure he was not dreaming a horrible nightmare. No, sure enough there was now a great wart on the right side of his face as well as on the left. The goblins had all disappeared and there was nothing for him to do but to return home.

The Farmer and the Boggart

Anon

The boggart lives under the ground in the north of England. He looks a little like a squat, hairy man with pointed teeth and arms as long as a rake. Now, once upon a time a man bought a piece of land. He went out to look at it, but as he was staring with pleasure at the good earth and planning what crop to plant, a boggart burst out of the earth in front of him and told him to go away. "Tis my land here," shrieked the boggart, "my land, my treasure, mine."

The farmer was a bold man and not afraid of the boggart. He suggested they went to see what the lawyers would say about that. The boggart didn't like the sound of that, for he had a fear of towns and houses, and suggested instead that they should share anything that grew on the land equally.

"Very well," said the farmer, "will you take what grows above the ground, or what grows beneath the ground? Only mind that you stick to your word, for I'll have no chopping and changing once we're settled."

The Farmer and the Boggart

The boggart thought about oats and corn and rye and peas, and settled to take what grows above the ground. So the farmer planted potatoes. When the time came to divide up the crop, the farmer had a fine store for his winter food, while all the boggart got was bitter leaves and tough stalks and no crop at all. So he made a great fuss and said that next year he would take whatever grew below the ground.

"Very well," said the farmer, "I'm suited if you are." He sowed his land with wheat, which grew a fine crop for the farmer to make his bread out of, while the boggart got nothing but muddy roots.

The boggart was very angry. He demanded that next year wheat must be sown again, but this time whoever could

mow the most with
their scythe should
get the whole crop.
"Very well," said
the farmer, "I'm
agreed if you are."
When the time
came for the wheat
to be mown, the
farmer went to the
field with his scythe.
He started at one corner
and the boggart started at the
other, but what the boggart didn't know
was that the farmer had stuck iron rods in
among the stalks of corn. These wore down
the boggart's strength and took all the sharp
edge off his scythe. So the boggart stopped

to drink and the boggart stopped to rest, but the farmer mowed steadily on. He cut more and more wheat till at last the boggart threw down his scythe in despair and said, "You may take the land. I'll have no more to do with it or you."

The farmer lived happily ever after but the boggart was never seen in that part of the country again.

How the Goblins Turned to Stone

William Elliot Griffis

The monster goblins that used to live in Holland were ugly, short fellows, very smart, quick in action and able to travel far in a second. They had big heads, green eyes and split feet, like cows. They were so ugly that they were ordered to live underground and never come out during the day. If they did, they would be turned to stone.

The ruler of the goblins lived beneath the

How the Goblins Turned to Stone

earth as the king of the underworld. His palace was made of gold and glittered with gems. All the goblins who worked in the mines and at the forges and anvils, making swords, spears, bells and jewels, obeyed him.

The most wonderful thing about these monsters was the way in which they made themselves invisible while at their mischief. This was a little red cap that every goblin possessed, and which he was careful never to lose, for while under it, no goblin could be seen by human eyes.

One night, as a dear old lady lay ill in her bed, a middle-sized goblin, with his red cap on, came through a crack into the room and stood at the foot of her bed. Just for mischief and to frighten her by making himself visible, he took off his red cap.

When the old lady saw the imp she cried out loudly, "Go away, go away." But the goblin monster only laughed at her.

Calling her daughter, Alida, the old lady whispered in her ear, "Bring me my wooden shoes straight away."

Rising up in her bed, the old lady hurled the heavy clogs, one after the other, at the goblin's head. At this, he started to get out through the crack and away, but just as he squeezed through, Alida snatched his red cap away. Twirling the little red cap around on her forefinger, a brilliant thought struck her. She went and told the men her plan, and they agreed to it. This was to gather hundreds of farmers, townfolk, boys and men together on the next moonlit night, and round up all the goblins in the town.

How the Goblins Turned to Stone

By pulling off their red caps and holding them till the sun rose, they would all be turned to stone.

Knowing that the goblin would come the next night to steal back his red cap, she left a note outside the crack telling him to bring several hundred goblins to the great moor at midnight the next day. There he would find the red cap on a bush. With his companions he could celebrate the return of the cap. In return, she asked the goblin to bring her a gold necklace.

The moonlit night came round and hundreds of the men gathered together. The plan was to move together in a circle towards the centre, where Alida was to hang the red cap upon a bush. Then, with a rush, the men were to snatch off all the goblins' caps, pulling and grabbing, whether they could see or feel anything or not.

The placing of the red cap upon the bush in the centre by Alida was the signal.

So when the great round-up narrowed to a small space, the men began to grab, snatch and pull. Putting their hands out in the air at the height of about a yard from the ground, they hustled and pushed hard. In a few minutes, hundreds of red caps were in their hands and as many goblins became visible. They were indeed an ugly collection.

But hundreds of other goblins escaped with their caps on and were still invisible. However, as they broke

Boggarts, Trolls and Goblins

148

How the Goblins Turned to Stone

away in groups they were seen, for in each bunch one or more fellow was visible because he wasn't wearing his cap. So the men divided into squads to chase the monsters. The racket kept up till the sky in the east was grey. The goblins were anxious to help their fellows or to get back their own caps, fearing the disgrace of returning bare-headed to their king and getting a good scolding. So before they even knew it was day, the sun suddenly rose on them. At the first ray of the sun, the goblins were all turned to stone.

The treeless, desolate land that, a moment before, was full of struggling goblins and men, became as quiet as the blue sky above. Nothing but some groups of rounded rocks and stones remained of the ugly goblins.

There these groups of rocks and stones, big and little, lie to this day. Among the buckwheat and the potato blossoms of the summer, under the shadows and clouds and whispering breezes of autumn, and covered with the snows of winter, they can be seen on deserted heaths.

Over some of the rocks and stones, oak trees, centuries old, have grown. Others are near or among the farmers' grain fields, or not far from houses and barnyards.

The cows wander and graze among the

How the Goblins Turned to Stone

groups of rocks and stones knowing nothing
of their past and how they got there.
  And the monster goblins come no more.

The Christmas Goblins

Charles Dickens

In an old abbey town a long, long while ago, there worked as sexton and gravedigger in the churchyard one Gabriel Grubb. He was a cross, surly fellow who mixed with nobody but himself and an old wicker bottle, which fitted into his large, deep waistcoat pocket.

A little before twilight one Christmas Eve, Gabriel put his spade on his shoulder, lit his

The Christmas Goblins

lantern and took himself towards the old churchyard. He had a grave to finish digging by the next morning and, feeling very low, he thought it might raise his spirits if he got on with his work at once.

Gabriel Grubb strode along until he turned into the dark lane that led to the churchyard. It was a gloomy, mournful place into which the townspeople did not care to go except in broad daylight, so he was very cross to hear a young boy roaring out some jolly song about having a merry Christmas.

Gabriel waited until the boy came up, then rapped him over the head with his lantern five or six times to teach him to lower his voice. As the boy hurried away with his hand to his head, Gabriel Grubb chuckled to himself and entered the churchyard, locking the gate behind him.

He took off his coat, put down his lantern and, getting into an unfinished grave, worked at digging it for an hour or so with strong determination.

But the earth was hardened with the frost, and it was no easy task to break it up and shovel it out.

At any other time this would have made Gabriel very miserable. However, he was so pleased at having stopped the small boy's singing that he took little heed of the small progress he had made when he finished work for the night.

Gabriel Grubb looked down into the grave with grim satisfaction. He murmured to himself as he gathered up his things,

The Christmas Goblins

"Brave lodgings for one, brave lodgings
   for one,
   A few feet of cold earth when life is
   done."
"Ho! ho!" he laughed, as he set himself
down on a flat tombstone, which was a
favourite resting place of his, and drew forth
his wicker bottle. "A coffin at Christmas. A
Christmas box. Ho! ho! ho!"

"Ho! ho! ho!" repeated a voice close
beside him.

"It was the echoes," said he, raising the
bottle to his lips again.

"It was not," said a deep voice.

Gabriel Grubb started up quickly and
stood rooted to the spot with terror, for his
eyes rested on a form that made his blood
run cold.

The Christmas Goblins

Seated on an upright tombstone close to him was a strange, unearthly figure. It was sitting perfectly still, grinning at Gabriel Grubb with such a grin as only a goblin could call up.

"What are you doing here on Christmas Eve?" said the goblin sternly.

"I came to dig a grave, sir," stammered Gabriel Grubb.

"What man wanders among graves on such a night as this?" cried the goblin.

"Gabriel Grubb! Gabriel Grubb!" screamed a wild chorus of voices that seemed to fill the churchyard.

"What have you got in that bottle?" said the goblin.

"Gin, sir," replied Gabriel, trembling more than ever.

"Who drinks gin alone, and in a churchyard on such a night as this?"

"Gabriel Grubb! Gabriel Grubb!" exclaimed the wild voices again.

"And who, then, is our lawful prisoner?" exclaimed the goblin, raising his voice.

The invisible chorus replied, "Gabriel Grubb! Gabriel Grubb!"

"Well, Gabriel, what do you say to this?" said the goblin, as he grinned a broader grin than before.

Gabriel Grubb gasped for breath.

"What do you think of this, Gabriel?"

"It's – it's very curious, sir, very curious, sir, and very pretty," replied Gabriel, half dead with fright. "But I think I'll go back and finish my work, sir, if you please."

"Work!" said the goblin, "What work?"

The Christmas Goblins

"The grave, sir."

"Oh! The grave, eh? Who makes graves at a time when other men are merry, and takes pleasure in it?"

Again the voices replied, "Gabriel Grubb! Gabriel Grubb!"

"I'm afraid my friends want you, Gabriel," said the goblin.

"I'm sorry, sir," replied the horror-stricken Gabriel, "I don't think they can. They don't know me, sir. I don't think the gentlemen have ever seen me."

"Oh! Yes, they have. We know the man who struck the boy in the bitterness of his heart because the boy could be merry and he could not."

Here the goblin gave a loud, shrill laugh, which the echoes returned.

"I – I am afraid I must leave you, sir," said Gabriel, making an effort to move.

"Leave us!" said the goblin, "Ho! ho! ho!"

As the goblin laughed, he suddenly darted towards Gabriel, laid his hand upon his collar and sank with him through the earth. When Gabriel had had time to fetch his breath he found himself in what appeared to be a large cavern, surrounded on all sides by goblins, ugly and grim.

"And now," said the King of the Goblins, seated in the centre of the room on an elevated seat, "show the man of misery and gloom the pictures from our storehouses."

As the goblin said this a cloud rolled gradually away and showed a small, barely furnished, but neat, apartment. Little children were gathered round a bright fire,

The Christmas Goblins

clinging to their mother's gown or playing round her chair. A simple meal was spread upon the table and a chair was placed near the fire. Soon the father entered and the children ran to meet him. As he sat down to his meal the mother sat by his side and all seemed happy and comfortable.

"So what do you think of that?"the goblin asked.

Gabriel murmured something about it being very pretty.

"Show him some more," said the goblin.

Many a time the cloud went and came, and many a lesson it taught to Gabriel Grubb. He saw that men who worked hard and earned their little bit of bread were cheerful and happy. He came to the conclusion that it was a very respectable sort of world after all. No sooner had he decided this than the cloud that closed over the last picture seemed to settle on his senses and lull him to rest. One by one the goblins faded from his sight and, as the last one disappeared, he sank to sleep.

The Christmas Goblins

The day had broken when Gabriel awoke and he found himself lying on the flat gravestone, with the wicker bottle empty by his side. He got to his feet as well as he could and, brushing the frost off his coat, turned towards the town.

But Gabriel Grubb was an altered man. He had learned lessons of gentleness and good nature by his strange adventures in the goblin's cavern.

The Goblin's Arm

William Elliot Griffis

Raiko and his brave companion, Tsuna, are great heroes in Japanese fairy tales. Onis are terrifying goblins or demons with horns on their heads and tusks in their mouths.

Under Captain Raiko were three brave guardsmen, one of whom was named Tsuna. The duty of these men-at-arms was to watch at the gates leading to the palace.

It had become dangerous in the city, so many good people were afraid to go out

The Goblin's Arm

into the streets at night. Worse than all else
was the report that hill-goblins, called onis
in Japan, were prowling around in the dark.
They would seize people by the hair of their
heads, then they would drag them away to
the mountains.

The worst place in the town, to which
the two-horned goblin came most often,
was at the south-western gate. To this post
of danger, Raiko sent Tsuna, the bravest of
his guards.

It was on a dark, rainy and dismal night
that Tsuna started, well-armed, to stand
guard at the gate. Tsuna's trusty helmet was
knotted over his chin and all the pieces of
his armour were well laced up. His sandals
were tight on his feet, and in his belt was
thrust his trusty sword, freshly sharpened

until its edge was like a razor's, and with it
he could cut in half a hair floating in the air.

Tsuna paced up and down the stone way
with his eyes and ears wide open. The wind
was blowing frightfully, the storm howled,
and the rain fell in such torrents that soon
the cords of Tsuna's armour and his tunic
were soaked through.

The great bronze bell of the temple on
the hill boomed out the hours one after
another, until a single stroke told Tsuna it
was the hour of midnight.

Two hours passed and still Tsuna was
wide awake. The storm had calmed, but it
was darker than ever. The hour of three
rang out and the soft mellow notes of the
temple bell died away.

The warrior, almost without knowing it,

The Goblin's Arm

grew sleepy and fell into a doze. Then he
started and woke up. Tsuna shook himself,
jingled his armour, pinched himself, and
even pulled out his little
knife and pricked his
leg with the point of
it to keep himself
awake, but all in
vain. Overcome by
drowsiness, he leant
against the gatepost
and fell asleep.

This was just what
the oni wanted. All
the time it had been
squatting on the cross-
piece at the top of the
gate waiting for his

opportunity. Now, the oni slid down as softly as a monkey and, with its iron-like claws, grabbed Tsuna by the helmet and began to drag him into the air.

In an instant Tsuna was awake. Seizing the goblin's hairy wrist with his left hand, he drew his sword with his right, swept it round his head and cut off the oni's arm. Frightened and howling with pain, the creature leapt from the post and disappeared into the clouds.

Tsuna waited with drawn sword in hand, but in a few hours it was morning. The sun rose on the pagodas and gardens and temples of the capital city. Everything was beautiful and bright. Tsuna returned to report to his captain, carrying the goblin's arm in triumph. Raiko examined it and praised Tsuna loudly for his bravery, then rewarded him with a silken sash.

Now, it is said that if a goblin's arm be cut off it can be joined with the body again if it is found within a week. So Raiko warned Tsuna to lock it up and watch it night and day, in case it is stolen from him.

Tsuna went to the stone-cutters and bought a strong box cut out of the solid stone. It had a heavy lid on it, which slid in a groove and came out only by touching a secret spring. Into this he put the arm. Then setting it in his bedchamber, he guarded it day and night, keeping the gate and all his doors locked. He didn't allow anyone who was a stranger to look at the trophy.

Six days passed by and Tsuna began to think he was safe, for all of his doors were tightly shut. So he set the box out in the middle of the room and sat down in ease before it. He took off his armour and put on his court robes. During the evening but rather late, there was a feeble knock, like that of an old woman, at the gate outside.

Tsuna cried out, "Who's there?"

The squeaky voice of his aunt, as it seemed, who was a very old woman, replied, "I want to see my nephew to praise him for his bravery in cutting the goblin's arm off."

So Tsuna let her in and carefully locked the door behind her. Tsuna helped her into the room, where she sat down on the mats in front of the box, very close to it. Then she grew talkative and praised Tsuna until he felt very proud.

All the time the old woman's left shoulder was covered with her dress, while her right hand was out. Finally she begged to be allowed to see the arm. Tsuna at first politely refused, but she urged until he slid back the stone lid just a little.

"This is my arm!" cried the old woman, turning into a goblin and dragging it out of the casket.

The goblin flew up to the ceiling and was out through the roof in a twinkling. Tsuna rushed out of the house to shoot it with an arrow, but he could just

The Goblin's Arm

see the goblin far off in the clouds, grinning
horribly. As he watched, he saw the cut-off
arm join again with the body, and the
goblin shook *both* fists at him in victory.

The Troll and the Bear

A traditional Norwegian tale

Once upon a time, in the olden days in Norway, there was a farm in the mountains where nobody could stay over on Christmas Eve. All the folk had to go down to the old farm in the valley and spend Christmas there. For every Christmas Eve an ugly troll came lumbering down from the high peaks with a sackful of toads on his back, and he made himself

The Troll and the Bear

comfortable in front of the farm's fire. There he would sit, toasting toads and popping them in his mouth. If anyone popped their head round the door, the troll would roar and rumble and threaten to tear them to pieces.

One time, just as the folk were leaving the farm, there came a man with a performing bear. They told him about the troll and advised him to get away from there. But the man was looking for shelter and begged to be allowed to stay. He was determined, so they finally gave him leave.

Towards the evening, the troll came to the farm with his sack on his back. He sat down by the fire, opened the sack and pulled out one toad after another. He took each one by its hind legs and held it over the fire till it was roasted, and then swallowed it. So one toad after the other went inside him for some time.

Then the troll turned to the man and, pointing to the bear, said, "What's your beast's name?"

"Toad," said the man.

The troll took a toad, roasted it and held it out to the bear, saying, "Toad shall have a toad." But as he did so, the man pinched the bear's arm and the bear growled and began to rise.

The Troll and the Bear

"Just you take care," said the man to the troll, "don't make him angry or he'll tear you into pieces."

The troll looked quite frightened and asked, "More like him?"

"No," said the man, "all the others are much bigger and fiercer than him."

"Where others?" said the troll.

"Oh," said the man. "They're coming up the hillside looking for their food."

The troll made haste to tie up the toads he had left in the sack. Then he threw it on his back and went out the door in a hurry.

Next morning, when the people of the farm came home, the man was lying in the bed and the bear beside the fire, both quite comfortable. When the man told them how he had got on they were very glad, and told

The Troll and the Bear

him to come again next Christmas Eve. He
did, but the troll did not come, and has
never shown himself there since.

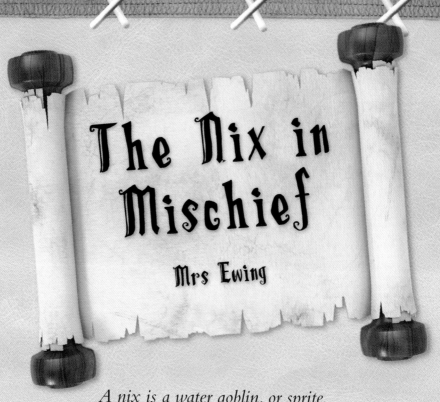

The Nix in Mischief

Mrs Ewing

A nix is a water goblin, or sprite,
that appears in many German folk tales.

A certain lake in Germany was once the
home of a nix, who became tired of life
underwater and decided to go into the
upper world to amuse himself.

His friends and relations all tried to
persuade him not to go. "Be wise," they said,
"and remain where you are safe. You have

no reason to leave the lake. Few of our kind have had dealings with the human race without suffering from their curiosity or clumsiness. Do them what good you may, but in the long run you won't get thanked for your deeds. Think how many lakes they have already banished us from. Leave them well alone and stay where you are."

But this advice did not please the nix and he only said, "I shall not expect gratitude, but I wish to amuse myself. The dwarves and goblins play whatever pranks they please on men and women and they do not always have the worst of it. When I hear of their adventures the soles of my feet tingle. Am I to be left out of the fun because I live in a lake instead of a hill?"

His friends repeated their warnings, but

the nix didn't listen. He spent his time dreaming of the clever tricks by which he should outwit the human race.

Shortly after this, a young girl came down to the lake to gather water to wash with. She dipped her pail in just above the nix's

The Nix in Mischief

head and in a moment he jumped in, and was carried safely to land.

The maid was Bess, the washerwoman's daughter. As she had had one good scolding that morning for oversleeping, and another about noon for being slow with her work, she took up the pail and set off home without delay.

Though she held it steadily enough, the bucket shook and the water spilled out. Thinking that her right arm might be tired, she moved the weight to her left but with no better success. The water still spilled out at every step. "One would think there were fishes in the pail," Bess said, as she set it down. But there was nothing to be seen but a thin, red water worm wriggling at the bottom. It was in this shape that the nix had disguised himself, and he almost wriggled out of his skin with delight at the success of his first attempt at mischief.

When they went forward once more, the nix leapt and jumped harder than ever, so that not only was the water spilled, but the girl's dress was soaked.

"The pail is bewitched!" cried the poor girl. "How my mother will scold me for this! My back aches as if I were carrying lead, and yet the water is nearly all gone."

"This is something like fun!" laughed the nix, and by the time they came to their journey's end, there was only a tiny bit of water in the pail.

"Was there ever a poor woman cursed with such a careless daughter?" cried the mother when she saw the dripping dress.

The Nix in Mischief

Meanwhile, the nix could hardly stop laughing. When the woman told Bess to warm some water quickly for the wash, he was in no way worried. He had never seen boiling water, and he slipped from the pail into the kettle.

"Now," cried the mother sharply, "see if you can lift that kettle without slopping water all over your clothes."

"Aye, aye," laughed the nix, "see if you can, my dear!" As poor Bess seized it in her sturdy red hands, he began to dance as before. But the kettle had a lid, which the pail had not. Bess was a strong, strapping lass and with an effort she set the kettle on the fire. "I shall be glad when I'm safely in bed," she muttered. "Everything has gone wrong today."

"It is warm in here," said the nix to himself after a while. "In fact – stuffy. But one must pay something for a frolic, and it tickles my ears to hear that old woman scolding her daughter for my pranks. It is worth a little discomfort, though it certainly is warm, and I think it is growing warmer."

The bottom of the kettle grew quite hot and burned the nix so that he had to jump up and down in the water to keep himself cool. The noise of this made the woman think that the kettle was boiling, and she began to scold her daughter as before, shouting, "Are you coming with that kettle tonight or not? The water is hot already."

This time the nix laughed (as they say) on the other side of his face, for the water had now become as hot as the bottom of the kettle, and he screamed at the top of his shrill tiny voice with pain.

"How the kettle sings tonight!" said Bess, "And how it rains!" she added. For at that moment a tremendous storm burst around the house and rain poured down in sheets of water, as if it meant to wash everything into the lake.

The kettle now really boiled and the lid danced up and down with the frantic leaping and jumping of the nix, who puffed and blew till his breath came out of the spout in clouds of steam.

"If your eyes were as sharp as your ears you'd see that the water is boiling over," snapped the woman. Giving her daughter a passing push, she hurried to the fireplace and lifted the kettle onto the ground.

But no sooner had she set it down, than the lid flew off and out jumped a little green water goblin. The nix ran straight out of the door, wringing his hands and crying, "Three hundred and three years have I lived in the water of this lake and I never knew it to boil before!"

As he crossed the threshold, a clap of thunder broke with what sounded like a peal of

The Nix in Mischief

laughter from many voices, and then the storm stopped as suddenly as it had begun.

The woman now saw what had happened. The next morning she did not fail to fasten an old horseshoe to the door of her house to keep the nixes out in future. And seeing that she had been unfair to her daughter, she bought her the prettiest set of pink ribbons that were to be found at the next fair.

Bess (who wasn't much bothered by a few sharp scoldings) thought this was the best bargain she had ever made. But whether the nix was equally well satisfied is not known.

The Widow's Son

Katharine Pyle

A Scandinavian tale

Once upon a time a poor lad set out to earn his living. He journeyed on a short way and a long way, and then came to a dark and gloomy wood. The lad had not gone far into it when he met a tall troll, as dark and gloomy as the wood itself, who said, "What are you doing here?"

"I am seeking work," answered the widow's son.

The Widow's Son

"Then come with me and I will give you enough to do but not too much," said the troll. They set out and travelled along, and after a while they came to a great, dark house set all alone in the midst of the wood. The troll showed the lad in and told him what to do.

The lad worked hard and pleased his new master, so after a few days the troll said, "I am going away on a journey. Until I return you may do as you please. But there is one part of the house you have never seen, and that is the three cellars. If you so much as open one of the doors, you will suffer for it."

"Why should I want to go into the cellars?" asked the lad. "The house and the yard are good enough for me."

The lad stayed at the house, and cleaned

and polished and ate and drank. 'I wonder what can be in those cellars that my master does not want me to see,' thought the lad. 'Not that I mean to look, but it does no harm to wonder about it.'

Every hour that the lad stayed there in the house alone he grew more curious about the cellars. At last he could bear it no longer. "I'll just take a wee peep into one of them," he said. "That can surely do no harm to anyone."

So he opened the cellar door and went down a flight of stone steps into the first cellar. He looked all about him. There was nothing at all there but a whip made of thorns lying on a shelf behind the door. "That is not much for the master to have made such a fuss about," said the lad.

The Widow's Son

Then he went on to the second cellar. He opened the door and looked about, but all he saw was a shelf behind the door, and on it was a water jug.

"There is not much to see and I wish I had not come," said the lad to himself.

Next he opened the third door and there was a magnificent coal-black horse chained to a manger, and the manger was filled with red-hot coals. At the horse's tail was a basket of hay.

"That is a cruel thing to do to an animal," cried the lad. He untied the horse from the manger and turned him so he could eat.

Then the black horse spoke to him in a human voice. "You have done a kind act," said the horse, "and you shall not suffer for it. If the Troll Master finds you here when he returns he will surely take your life, and that must not be. Promise to do exactly what I say and you shall be safe. Take the

The Widow's Son

thorn whip and the jug of water. Then
mount my back and ride. If the Troll Master
finds us here when he returns, it will be
terrible for both of us."

The lad did as the horse told him. He
took the thorn whip and the jug of water,
and mounted the black horse's back. The
horse carried him up the steps, out of the
house and fast, fast away through the forest
and over the plains beyond.

After a while the black horse said, "I hear
a noise behind us. Look and see whether
anyone is coming."

The lad turned and looked. "Yes, yes, it is
the master," he said, "and with him is a
whole crowd of people."

"They are his troll friends," said the horse.
"Throw the thorn whip behind us, but be

195

sure you throw it clear and do not let
it touch even the tip of my tail."
    The lad threw the thorn whip
behind him and at
once a great forest
of thorns grew up

where it fell. No one could have forced a way through it. The troll and his friends had to go home and get clubs and axes to cut a path through.

By this time the horse had gone a long, long way. Then he said to the lad, "Look back and see whether you see anyone, for I hear a noise behind us."

The lad looked back. "I see the master coming," he said, "and a great number of monsters with him."

"Yes, yes," said the horse. "He has all of his friends with him now. We must not let them catch us. Pour the water from the jug behind us, but be careful that none of it touches me."

The lad stretched back his arm and poured the water out from the jug, but his haste was such that three drops fell upon the horse's flanks. Immediately a great lake rose about them, and because of the three drops that had fallen on the horse, the lake was not only behind them but about them, and the horse had to swim for it.

The trolls came to the edge of the lake. As there was no way to cross over, they threw themselves down on their stomachs and began to drink it up. They drank and they drank and they drank, until at last they all burst.

The horse went on until he came to a wood and there he stopped. "Get down now," he said to the lad, "then take your sword and cut off my head."

The Widow's Son

When the lad heard this he was horrified. "What is this you ask of me?" he cried. "All that I have I owe to you. How could I in return do you such an injury?"

But the black horse reminded the lad that he had promised. The youth could not refuse after that. He drew his sword and cut off the horse's head. At once, instead of a coal-black horse, a handsome young prince stood before him. The lad could barely believe his eyes. He stared about him, wondering what had become of the horse.

"There is no need to look for the black horse," said the stranger, "for I am he." He then told the lad that he was the son of the king of a neighbouring country. An enemy had risen up and slain the king, and had given the prince to the troll, who had turned him into a horse and taken him away to his castle. "You have rescued me from the enchantment and now I am free to claim my land again," said the prince.

After that the lad and the prince rode to the prince's own country. His people received him with joy, and he and the lad lived in the greatest friendship forever after.

The Troll Who Wrote a Letter

A traditional Scandinavian tale

Once upon a time a troll set up his home near the village of Kund, in a high bank where he had scrabbled out a cave to live in. However the people of the village, not knowing he was there, built a church on the land above his bank. This made the old troll very cross. The bells ringing in the steeple at all hours and the bustle of people coming and going from the church troubled

The Troll Who Wrote a Letter

him dreadfully. All trolls hate the sound of bells ringing. In the end he decided to leave his home and find one in some country without any village or church.

The troll travelled out into the wilds where he made his home among the swamps and bushes. But he hated the people of Kund for forcing him out of his home.

Now, a man who had lately settled in the village of Kund came past the swamp and met this troll on the road. It was late at night and he didn't notice that the troll was not a man like himself.

"Where do you live?" asked the troll.

The man answered him truthfully and said, "I am from the town of Kund."

The troll had been waiting for a chance like this to get his revenge on the village.

"So," said the troll, "I don't know you then. And yet I think I know every man in Kund. Will you be so kind as to take a letter for me back with you to Kund?"

The man said he would gladly do so. The troll took a letter out of his pocket and said, "I beg you then, to take this letter to

The Troll Who Wrote a Letter

Kund, not removing it from your pocket until you get there. And when you get there, throw it over the churchyard wall. The person it is for will expect it there."

'What a strange way to deliver a letter' thought the man. But he agreed to do what he was asked.

The troll then went away in great haste, and with him the letter went entirely out of the man's mind. But when he was halfway along the road, the man sat down by the meadow where Tiis lake now is to eat his bread and cheese. He suddenly remembered the troll's letter and the strange instructions that went with it. He felt a great curiosity to look at the letter, even though he had promised not to take it out of his pocket.

'I won't open it' he thought, 'but no harm

can come from just
looking at the outside.'

So he took the letter out of his pocket
and sat a while with it in his hands.
Suddenly a little water began to dribble out
from beneath the seal. The letter now
unfolded itself and the water came out faster
and faster, pouring in great waves out of the

The Troll Who Wrote a Letter

letter. The poor man had to scramble for his life, and only just got away safely. The wicked troll, hoping to drown the church, had enclosed a whole lake in the letter.

The troll had thought he would get revenge on Kund church by destroying it in this way. But God ordered it so that the lake ran out in the great meadow, where Tiis lake now stands.

GRUESOME GIANTS AND AWFUL OGRES

Giant Tom and Giant Blubb

William Elliot Griffis

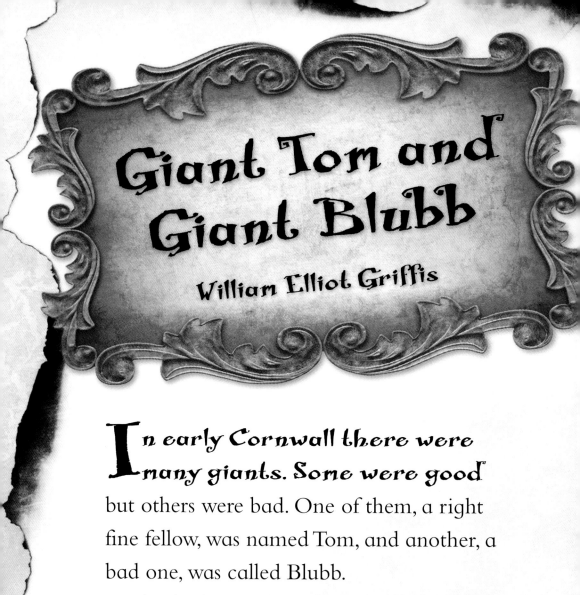

In early Cornwall there were many giants. Some were good but others were bad. One of them, a right fine fellow, was named Tom, and another, a bad one, was called Blubb.

This bad giant had had twenty wives and was awfully cruel. Nobody ever knew what became of the twenty maidens he had married. Sometimes people called this big fellow Giant Blunderbuss, but Blubb was his name for short. He was mostly made up of head and stomach, for his main thought was to eat. His skull was as big as a market wagon loaded with carrots, but most people believed a coconut would hold all the brains he had.

Giant Blubb had built a mighty castle between a big hill and a river. Under it were cellars of great size filled with treasures of many kinds – gold, silver, jewels and gems. To guard his underground treasures, Giant Blubb had two huge and fierce dogs, supposed to be named Catchem and Tearem. But the names their master really called them by was a secret. Yet anyone who had a piece of meat ready to throw to them and knew their real names, which were passwords, could quieten them. Then they could walk right by the dogs and get the treasures.

Besides these dogs, the only living thing in the castle when the giant went out was the latest Mrs Blubb. Yet she was in constant fear for her life, thinking that her big husband would make a meal out of her sometime soon.

What made all the country hate this cruel giant was not just his awful appetite. It was because he had ruined the King's Highway. When Giant Blubb wanted to make his castle bigger, he had the walls and towers built down to the river's edge. This closed off the highway so that people had to go far around and up over the hill, or by boat along the river. Such a round about way took much time and trouble for all.

Everybody had to put up with it until Giant Tom came along. His real name was Rolling Stone, for he never stuck long in one place at a job and didn't care for money or fine clothes.

This jolly fellow was very good-natured and popular, but often lazy. However, as he could do six men's work when he put his mind to it – as often he did – he was always welcome. In fact, he was too popular for his own good.

One day, when ten fellows were trying to lift a big, long log onto a cart and were unable to do it, Tom came along and told

them to stand back. Then he hoisted the log
onto the cart, roped it into place and told
the cartman to drive on. All the fellows
cheered him and one of them lifted his cap
and cried out, "Hurrah for Giant Tom. He's
the fellow to whip Giant Blubb."

"He is! He is!" they all cried
out in chorus.

"Who is this Giant Blubb?
Where does he live?" asked
Tom, rolling up his sleeves.

Then they told Tom the
story of how the big bully
had ruined the King's
Highway by building a great
wall and tower across the
road to shut it off.

"Never mind, boys. I'll see to

him," said Tom. "Leave the matter with me."

The next day, Giant Tom went into town and hired himself out to drive a wagon. He asked the boss to give him the route that led past Giant Blubb's castle, over the King's Highway.

The boss said, "Go ahead, my boy. I'll pay you double wages if you will open that road again."

Tom drove off. He occupied all the room on the seat of the cart, which two men usually filled and left plenty of room on either side.

Cracking his whip, the driver kept the four horses at a galloping pace. Very soon he called out, "Whoa," before the curved high gateway of Giant Blubb.

Tom shouted from the depth of his lungs,

"Open the gate and let me drive through. This is the King's Highway."

For a minute, the only reply was the barking of the dogs. Then a rattling of bolts was heard and the great gates swung open.

"Who are you, you rude fellow? Go round over the hill or I'll thrash you," shouted Giant Blubb in a rage.

"Better save your breath, you big boaster, and come out and fight," said Tom.

"Fight? You dwarf. I'll just get a stick and whip you, as I would a bad boy."

Giant Blubb stepped aside into the grove nearby, all the while keeping an eye on his gate, guarded by his two monstrous dogs. He chose an elm tree twenty feet high, tore it up by the roots, pulled off the branches and peeled it for a whip. Meanwhile, Giant

Giant Tom and Giant Blubb

Tom turned over the wagon, pulled out its
longest plank and took off one of the
wheels. Then, as if armed with a spear and
shield, he advanced to meet Giant Blubb.
Giant Tom whistled like a boy as he
marched forwards.

Giant Blubb lifted his elm whip to strike,

but Tom warded off the blow with his wheel shield. Then he punched him in the stomach with the plank, so hard that the big fellow slipped and rolled over in the mud.

Picking himself up, Giant Blubb, now half blind with rage, rushed towards Giant Tom, who, this time, made a lunge that knocked Giant Blubb over.

But Tom was not a cruel fellow and had no desire to kill anyone. So he threw down his plank and wheel.

But instead of thanking Tom, Giant Blubb rushed at him again. He was in too much of a rage to see anything clearly, while Tom, perfectly cool, gave the angry giant a kick in the stomach. Giant Blubb fell down again and rolled on the ground. Then Tom sent the giant on his way.

Giant Tom and Giant Blubb

Tom made himself owner of Giant Blubb's castle and all its treasures. He opened the King's Highway again, made sure his aging mother had all she needed, and was always kind to the sick and poor.

In Cornwall today, they still tell stories of the big fellow who got rid of Giant Blubb's gate.

Buchettino

Thomas Frederick Crane

Once upon a time there was a child whose name was Buchettino. One morning his mamma called him and said, "Buchettino, will you do me a favour? Go and sweep the stairs." Buchettino, who was very obedient, did not wait to be told a second time, but went at once to sweep the stairs.

After sweeping all around, he found a

penny. Then he said to himself, "What shall I do with this penny? I have half a mind to buy some dates… but no! For I should have to throw away the stones. I will buy some apples… no! I will not, for I should have to throw away the core. I will buy some nuts… but no! For I should have to throw away the shells. What shall I buy, then? I will buy – I will buy – enough! I will buy a pennyworth of figs."

No sooner said than done. Buchettino bought a pennyworth of figs and went and sat up in a tree to eat them. While he was eating, an ogre passed by. Seeing Buchettino eating figs in the tree, the ogre said, "Buchettino, my dear Buchettino, give me a little fig with your dear little hand. If you don't, I will eat you!"

Buchettino threw the ogre a fig, but it fell in the dirt. The ogre repeated, "Buchettino, my dear Buchettino, give me a little fig with your dear little hand. If you don't, I will eat you!"

Then Buchettino threw him another, which also fell in the dirt. The ogre said again, "Buchettino, my dear Buchettino, give me a little fig with your dear little

Buchettino

hand. If you don't, I will eat you!"

Poor Buchettino. He did not see the trick and did not know that the ogre was trying to get him into his bag and eat him up.

What does Buchettino do? He leans down and foolishly gives the ogre a fig with his little hand.

The ogre, who wanted nothing better, suddenly grabbed Buchettino by the arm and put him into his bag. Then he put the bag on his back and headed for his home, crying, "Wife, my wife, put the kettle on the fire, for I have caught Buchettino!

Wife, my wife, put the kettle on the fire, for I have

caught Buchettino!"

When the ogre was near his house he put the bag on the ground and went off to attend to something else. Buchettino, with a knife that he had in his pocket, cut the bag open in a moment, filled it with large stones and then said, "My legs, run away for we need to go."

When the rascal of an ogre returned he picked up the bag and scarcely had he arrived home when he said to his wife, "Tell me, my wife, have you put the kettle on the fire?" She answered at once, "Yes."

"Then," said the ogre, "we will cook Buchettino. Come here and help me." Taking the bag, they carried it to the hearth to throw poor Buchettino into the kettle, but instead they found only the stones. Imagine how cheated the ogre felt. He was so angry that he bit his hands. The ogre could not bear the thought of losing Buchettino, and he swore to find him again and get his revenge.

So the next day, the ogre began to go all about the city and to look in all the hiding places. At last he happened to raise his eyes and saw Buchettino on a balcony, laughing so hard that his mouth stretched from ear to ear. The ogre thought he should burst with rage, but he pretended not to be angry and in a very sweet tone he said, "Buchettino, tell me, how did you manage to climb up there?"

Buchettino answered, "Do you really want to know? Then listen. I put dishes upon dishes, glasses upon glasses, pans upon pans, kettles upon kettles. Afterwards I climbed up on them and here I am."

"Ah! Is that so?" said the stupid ogre. "Then wait a bit!" And quickly he took so many dishes, glasses, pans and kettles, and made a great mountain of them. Then he began to climb up to try and catch Buchettino. But when he was nearly on the top – *crash!* –

Buchettino

everything fell down. That rascal of an
ogre fell down on the stones and was
cheated again. The ogre was so
cross he went off to another
country and never troubled
Buchettino again.

Then Buchettino, very
pleased with himself, ran
home to his mamma.

Brabo and the Giant

William Elliot Griffis

Ages ago, when the giants were numerous on the earth, there lived a big fellow named Antigonus. This giant was rough and cruel. He built a strong castle on the Scheldt River in Belgium, where the city of Antwerp now stands. The castle had four sides and high walls, and deep down in the earth were dark, damp dungeons.

Brabo and the Giant

Now, the river on which the giant built his castle was very grand, deep and wide. The captains of ships liked to sail on it because there was no danger from rocks and the country through which it flowed was so pretty.

Every day, one could see hundreds of white-sailed craft moving towards the sea or coming in from the ocean. The incoming ships brought sugar, wine, oranges, lemons, olives and other good things to eat, and wool to make warm clothes.

But one day, the wicked giant came into the country to stop the ships and make the captains pay him money. He strode through the town with a big knotted club made out of an oak tree. He cried out to all the people to assemble in the great open square.

Gruesome Giants and Awful Ogres

"From this day forth," he roared, "no ship shall pass by this place without my permission. Every captain must pay me. Whoever refuses shall have both his hands cut off and thrown into the river."

With this, the giant swung and twirled his club in the air and

then brought it down on a poor
countryman's cart, smashing it into pieces.

Now, there was a brave young fellow
named Brabo, who lived in the province of
Brabant. He studied the giant's castle and
saw a window where he could climb up
and get into the giant's chamber.

Brabo went to the Duke and promised
that if his lord's soldiers would storm the
gates of the castle, he would seek out and
fight the giant. While the soldiers battered
down the gates, he would climb the walls.
"He's nothing but a bully and a boaster,"
said Brabo.

The Duke agreed. On a dark night, one
thousand of his best men-at-arms marched
towards the giant's castle, but with no
drums or trumpets or anything that could

make a noise.

Reaching a wood full of big trees near the castle, Brabo and the soldiers waited till after midnight. All the dogs in the town and country for five miles around were seized and put into barns, so as not to bark and wake the giant up. They were given plenty to eat, so they quickly fell asleep and were perfectly quiet.

At the given signal, hundreds of men holding ships' masts or tree trunks marched against the castle gates. They punched and pounded, and at last smashed the iron-bound timbers and rushed in. At about the same time, the barn doors where the dogs had been kept were thrown open. In full cry, hundreds of the animals, from puppies to hounds, were at once out, barking, howling and yelping, as if they knew what was going on and wanted to see the fun.

But where was the giant? None of the captains could find him. Not one of the prisoners held in the castle or the soldiers could tell where he had hidden.

Brabo was not afraid. Some of his comrades outside helped him to set up a tall ladder against the wall. Then, while all the watchers and men-at-arms had gone to defend the gates, Brabo climbed into the castle through a slit in the thick wall. This had been cut out, like a window, for the bow-and-arrow men. Sword in hand, Brabo made for the giant's own room.

Glaring at the youth, the big fellow seized his club and brought it down with such force that it went through the wooden floor. But Brabo dodged the blow and, in a moment, made a sweep with his sword. Cutting off the giant's head, he threw it out the window. It had hardly touched the ground before the dogs arrived. One of the largest of these ran away with the trophy, and the big, ugly head of the bully was never found again.

Very soon, every house in Antwerp displayed lighted candles and the city was lit up. After this, thousands of ships from many countries loaded and unloaded their cargoes at the quays or sailed peacefully by.

Brabo and the Giant

Antwerp became rich again. The people loved their native city so dearly that they made the proverb: 'All the world is a ring, and Antwerp is the pearl set in it'.

Odysseus and the Cyclops

Andrew Lang

The Greek hero, Odysseus, is sailing with his men back from Troy to his own country. They have stopped at an island to get food and water.

When they were near the shore they saw a great cave by the sea. It was roofed in with green laurel branches, and seemed to be meant as a place to shelter sheep and goats. Round about it a high outer wall was built with

236

stones, and tall, leafy pines and oak trees.

In this cave, all alone with his flocks and herds, lived a huge, hideous Cyclops who was called Polyphemus.

Leaving some of his men to guard the ship, Odysseus took his best warriors with him and went to explore the one-eyed giant's cave. With him he carried a goat-skin full of precious wine that was dark red, sweet and strong.

Soon they came to the cave, but Polyphemus was not there. He had taken his flocks of sheep off to graze in the green meadows, leaving pens full of lambs and kids in the cave.

Towards evening, Polythemus came, driving his flocks before him and carrying a huge load of firewood on his back. He cast it down on the floor with a thunderous noise. Odysseus and his men fled in fear and hid themselves in the darkest corners of the cave. When Polyphemus had driven his sheep inside, he lifted from the ground a rock so huge that twenty-two four-wheeled wagons could not have carried it. With it, the giant blocked the doorway. Then he lit a fire and, when the flames lit up the dark-

Odysseus and the Cyclops

walled cave, he spied Odysseus and his men.

"Strangers, who are you?" he asked, in his great, rumbling voice. "Are you merchants or are you sea robbers?"

The sound of the giant's voice and the sight of his hideous face filled the men's hearts with terror, but Odysseus answered, "We come from Troy, driven here by winds and waves."

Polyphemus said nothing in reply, but sprang up and grabbed hold of two of the men. He ate the two men, bones and all, as if he had been a starving lion. When he had finished his meal, he stretched himself on the ground beside his sheep and goats, and slept.

Helpless and horrified, Odysseus and his men had watched the dreadful sight, but when the giant slept they began to make plans for their escape. All night they thought what they should do.

The next morning at dawn, Polyphemus awoke. He lit a fire, milked his flocks and gave each ewe her lamb. Next, he lifted the stone from the door, drove the flocks out and set the stone back again. Then, with a loud shout, he turned his sheep and goats towards the hills and left Odysseus and his remaining men imprisoned in the cave, plotting and planning how to get away.

At last Odysseus thought of a plan. By the sheep pen there lay a huge club of green olive wood, which Polyphemus had cut and was keeping until it should be dry enough to use as a staff. From this club, Odysseus cut a large piece and gave it to his men to fine down and make smooth.

Odysseus and the Cyclops

While they did this, Odysseus himself sharpened it to a point and hardened the point in the fire.

When the stake was ready, they hid it among the rubbish on the floor of the cave. In the evening, Polyphemus came down from the hills with his flocks and drove them all inside the cave. From the shadows of the cave Odysseus stepped forwards, holding in his hands an ivy bowl full of the dark red, sweet wine.

"Drink wine," said Odysseus, "and see what drink we carried on our ship."

Polyphemus quickly gulped down the strong wine.

"Give me more," he cried. "And tell me your name, stranger."

Again and again, Odysseus gave him the

241

bowl full of wine, until the strong wine went to the giant's head and made him stupid.

Then Odysseus said, "You asked me my name. Noman is my name, and Noman is what they call me."

The giant answered, "I will eat your friends first, Noman, and you last of all. That shall be my thanks for the wine."

Soon the wine made the giant so sleepy that he sank backwards with his great face upturned and fell fast asleep.

As soon as the giant slept, Odysseus thrust the stake he had prepared into the fire to make it red-hot. Then he drew the red-hot stake out and thrust it into the giant's eye.

With a great and terrible cry the giant sprang to his feet, and

Odysseus and the Cyclops

Odysseus and the others ran to hide. Mad with pain, he called to the other one-eyed giants, who lived in their caves on the hilltops. The giants, hearing his horrid yells, rushed to help him.

"What is the trouble, Polyphemus?" they asked. "Who is hurting or killing you?"

From the other side of the great stone Polyphemus shouted out, "Noman is hurting me."

Then the one-eyed giants said, "If no man is hurting you, then it must be an illness that makes you cry so loud, and this you must bear by yourself, for we cannot help you."

With that they strode away from the cave and left the blind giant groaning and roaring with pain. Groping with his hands,

Odysseus and the Cyclops

Polyphemus found the great stone that blocked the door. He lifted it away and sat himself down in the mouth of the cave with his arms stretched out. Sitting there, he fell asleep and, as soon as he slept, Odysseus planned and plotted how best to escape.

The rams of the giant's flocks were great, strong beasts, with thick and woolly fleeces. Odysseus tied them together in threes, and under the middle ram of each three, he tied one of his men. For himself, he kept the best ram of the flock. Odysseus curled himself underneath this ram and clung to it, his face upwards.

When dawn came, the rams went out of the cave door to the hills and green meadows. As each sheep passed Polyphemus, he felt along its back, but never guessed that the remaining men were bound beneath the thick-fleeced rams. Last of all came the young ram to which Odysseus clung.

The ram slowly walked on past the savage giant, towards the meadows near the sea. And soon they were far enough from the cave for Odysseus to let go of the ram and to stand up.

"There is no time to weep," said Odysseus, and he made his men hurry on board the ship, driving the giant's sheep before them.

Soon they were all on board, and the grey sea water was rushing off their oars as they sailed away very quickly from the land of the one-eyed giants.

Their hearts were sore because they had

Odysseus and the Cyclops

lost brave men of their company, but they were also glad that men had been saved from death at the hands of the Cyclops.

Jack in Wales

Flora Annie Steel

Once upon a time, Jack, the famous Giant Killer, found himself lost in wild Wales, far from any human house. As night fell he wandered on, until, on entering a narrow valley, he came to a very large, dreary-looking house, almost a castle, standing alone.

Being anxious for shelter Jack went up to the door and knocked. You may imagine his surprise and alarm when the summons was answered by a giant with two heads. But though this giant's look was very fierce, his manners were quite polite. The truth was that he was an evil giant. He appeared friendly because this was how he tried to win people over, by a show of false friendship.

So he welcomed Jack heartily in a strong Welsh accent and prepared a bedroom for him, where he was left with kind wishes for a good rest.

However, Jack was too tired to sleep well and, as he lay awake, he overheard the giant muttering to himself in the next room. Jack had very keen ears and he was able to make out these words, or something like them:

"Though here you lodge with me
    this night,
You shall not see the morning light.
   My club shall dash your brains outright."
   "Do you say!" said Jack,
starting up
at once.

"So that is your trick, is it? But I will be
even with you." Then, leaving his bed, Jack
laid a big piece of wood among the

blankets and, taking one of these to keep himself warm, made himself snug in a corner of the room. He pretended to snore, so as to make the giant think he was asleep.

And sure enough, in came the giant on tiptoe, carrying a big club. Then – *WHACK! WHACK! WHACK!*

Jack could hear the bed being beaten until the giant, thinking every bone of his guest's body must be broken, went out of the room again. Then Jack went calmly to bed once more and slept soundly.

Next morning the giant couldn't believe his eyes when he saw Jack coming down the stairs fresh and hearty.

"Odds splutter hur nails!" he cried astonished. "Did you sleep well? Was there nothing you felt in the night?"

"Oh," replied Jack, laughing in his sleeve, "I think a rat did come and give me two or three flaps of his tail."

The giant was dumbfounded. He led Jack to breakfast, brought him a bowl that held at least four gallons of porridge, and told him to eat the lot.

Jack in Wales

When Jack was travelling he wore a leather bag under his cloak to carry his things and, as it happened, he still had it with him. So, quick as thought, he hitched it round in front with the opening just under his chin.

Then he set to work at the mighty bowl, filled to the brim with grey, lumpy porridge. As he spooned up the mixture, he slipped the best part of it into the leather bag without the giant being any the wiser.

So they sat down to breakfast, the giant gobbling down his own measure of porridge, while Jack carried on with his.

"Now see," says crafty Jack when he had finished. "I'll show you a trick," and with that he stood up with a carving-knife, ripped up the leather bag and out fell all

GRUESOME GIANTS AND AWFUL OGRES

the porridge on the floor!

"Odds splutter hur nails!" cried the giant. Not to be outdone, he said, "I can do that myself!" He seized the carving-knife, ripped open his own belly and fell down dead.

And so Jack got rid of the Welsh giant.

The Three Little Pigs and the Ogre

Howard Pyle

There were once three nice, fat little pigs. The first was small, the second was smaller and the third was the smallest of all. These three little pigs thought of going out into the woods to gather acorns, for there were better acorns there than here.

"There's a great ogre who lives over in the woods," said the barnyard cock.

The Three Little Pigs and the Ogre

"And he will eat you up, body and bones," said the speckled hen.

"And that will be the end of you," said the black drake.

"If folks only knew what was good for them, they would stay at home," said the grey goose.

But the smallest of all the little pigs wanted to go out into the woods whether there was an ogre or not. So out into the woods he went.

The smallest little pig hunted for acorns here and there, and who should he meet but the great, wicked ogre himself.

"Aha!" the ogre said, "It is a nice, plump little pig that I have been wanting for my supper these last few days. So you will just come along with me now."

The little pig said he would go, but he asked the ogre if he had come across three fellows tramping about in the woods.

The ogre said he had met nobody in the woods that day.

"Dear, dear," said the smallest little pig, "but that is a pity, for those three fellows were three wicked robbers. They have just hidden a bag full of money in that hole up in the tree."

You can guess how the ogre pricked up his ears at this and how he stared till his eyes were as big as saucers.

"Just wait," said he to the smallest little pig, "I will be down again in a minute." So the ogre laid his jacket to one side and he climbed up the tree, up and up a long way, for he wanted to find that bag of money and he meant to keep it.

"Do you see the hole?" said the smallest of the little pigs.

The ogre said he could see the hole.

"And do you see the money?" the smallest of the little pigs asked.

The ogre said he could not see the money.

"Then, goodbye," said the smallest of the little pigs, and off he trotted home, leaving the ogre to climb down the tree.

"At least now you will go out into the woods no more," said the cock, the speckled hen, the black drake and the grey goose.

Well, there was no telling what the three little pigs would do – they would have to wait and see.

Next day, it was the middle-sized little pig who wanted to go out into the woods, for he also wanted to taste the acorns there.

So out into the woods the middle-sized little pig went, and there he had all the acorns that he wanted.

But the ogre came along. "Aha!" he said. "Now I have a plump pig for my supper for sure and certain."

But the middle-sized little pig just stood and looked at a great rock in front of him.

The Three Little Pigs and the Ogre

"Sh-h-h-h-h-h!" he said, "I am not to be talked to or bothered now!"

And why was the middle-sized pig not to be talked to or bothered? That was what the ogre really wanted to know.

The middle-sized little pig said he was looking at what was going on under the great rock, for he could see the little fairy folk brewing more beer than thirty-seven men could drink.

The ogre said he would like to see that for himself.

"Very well," said the middle-sized little pig, "there is nothing easier than to learn that trick. Just take a handful of leaves from that bush and rub them over your eyes. Then shut your eyes tight and count to fifty."

The ogre said he would have a try at that. So he gathered a handful of the leaves and rubbed them over his eyes, just as the middle-sized pig had said.

The Three Little Pigs and the Ogre

"And now are you ready?" said the middle-sized little pig.

The ogre said he was ready.

"Then shut your eyes and count," said the middle-sized little pig.

So the ogre shut his eyes as tightly as he could and began to count, "One, two, three, four, five," and so on. And while he was counting, the little pig was running away home again.

Now it was the largest of the three little pigs who began to talk about going out into the woods to look for acorns.

"You had better stay at home and take things as they come." That was what the cock, the speckled hen, the black drake and the grey goose said.

But the little pig wanted to go out into

the woods, and into the woods the little pig would go, ogre or no ogre.

After he had eaten all of the acorns that he wanted he began to think of

going home again, but just then the ogre came stomping along.

264

The Three Little Pigs and the Ogre

"Aha!" he said, "You shall just come
along home with me and tomorrow you
shall be made into sausages! There is to be
no trickery this time."

"Come, come!" said the largest little pig,
sitting back on his heels and regarding the
furious ogre quite calmly. "No need to be
so angry. I'm willing to do anything you
want. If it is sausages that you're after,
maybe I can help you. At the farm is a
storehouse filled with more sausages and
good things than two men can count. There
is a window where you could just squeeze
through. Only you must promise to eat
what you want and to carry nothing away
with you."

Well, the ogre liked the idea of that very
much. He promised to eat all he wanted in

the storehouse and to take nothing away with him, just as the pig had said. And so off they went together.

They came to the storehouse at the farm, and sure enough, there was a window. It was just large enough for the ogre to squeeze through without a button to spare in the size.

Dear, dear! How the ogre did stuff himself with the sausages and puddings and other good things in the storehouse.

Then the little pig bawled out as loud as he could, "Have you had enough yet?"

"Hush-sh-sh-sh-sh-sh!" said the ogre, "Don't talk so loud, or you'll be rousing the folks and having them about our ears like a hive of bees."

"No," bawled the little pig, louder than

before, "but tell me, have you had enough to eat yet?"

"Yes, yes," said the ogre, "I have had almost enough, only be quiet about it!"

"Very well!" bawled the little pig, as loud as he could, "If you have had enough, and if you have eaten all of the sausages and all of the puddings you can, it is about time that you were going. For here comes the farmer and two of his men to see what all the noise is about."

And sure enough, the farmer and his men were coming as fast as they could.

When the ogre heard them coming, he felt sure that it was time that he must be getting away home again. He tried to get out of the same window that he had got in a little while before. But he had stuffed

himself with so much of the good things
that he had swelled, and there he stuck in
the storehouse window like a cork in a
bottle, and could budge neither one way
nor the other.

The Three Little Pigs and the Ogre

"Oho!" said the farmer, "You were after my sausages and my puddings, were you? Then you will come no more."

And that was so, for when the farmer and his men were done with the ogre, he never went into the woods again.

As for the three little pigs, they trotted into the woods every day of their lives, for there was nobody to stop them from gathering all the acorns that they wanted.

Thor's Adventures among the Giants

Julia Goddard

From *Wonderful Stories from Northern Lands*

*Thor is the son of Odin, the Norse king
of the Gods. Loki is Thor's mischievous companion.*

Once upon a time Thor set out
upon his travels, taking Loki
with him. They set off together in Thor's
chariot, drawn by its two strong male goats.

They could just see a dark forest in the
far distance. One or two huge rocks and
great blocks of stone were scattered about.

Thor's Adventures among the Giants

They pushed on and soon found that they were in a land where no men lived. The darkness became so deep by the time they reached the forest, that they only knew they had arrived there because Loki hit his head against a low branch.

Soon after this, Thor cried out, "Good luck! I have found a house. Follow close after me and we will make ourselves comfortable for the night."

They groped their way along the wall, seeking to find an entrance. At last Thor found a huge entrance opening into a wide hall. Passing through this they turned to the left into a large room that was quite empty. Here, after eating some food, they stretched themselves upon the hard floor and fell asleep.

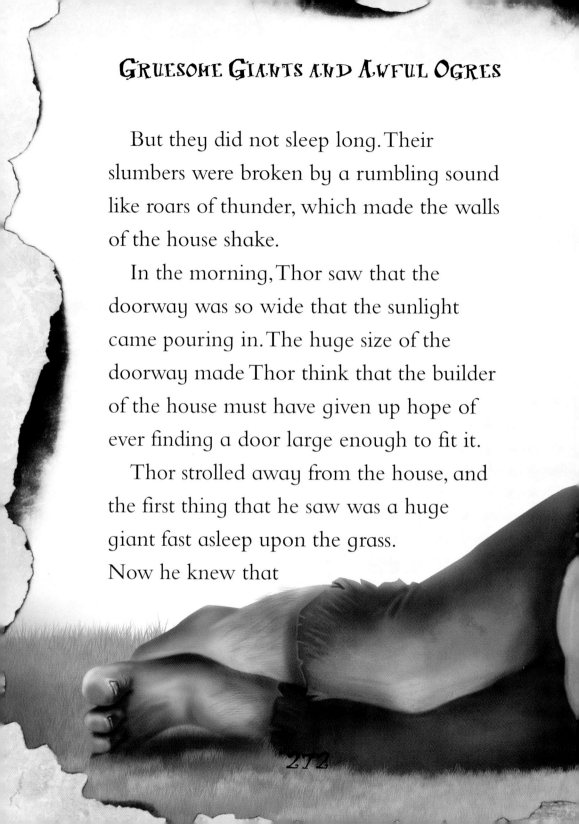

But they did not sleep long. Their slumbers were broken by a rumbling sound like roars of thunder, which made the walls of the house shake.

In the morning, Thor saw that the doorway was so wide that the sunlight came pouring in. The huge size of the doorway made Thor think that the builder of the house must have given up hope of ever finding a door large enough to fit it.

Thor strolled away from the house, and the first thing that he saw was a huge giant fast asleep upon the grass. Now he knew that

the thunder that had frightened them in the
night had been nothing more or less than
the loud snoring of the giant.

At that moment the giant woke up and
Thor asked, "What is your name?"

"My name," said the giant, raising
himself on one elbow, "is Skrymner. You, I
believe, are the god Thor?"

"I am," answered
the god.

"Do you happen to have picked up my glove?" asked the giant carelessly.

Then Thor knew that what he and his companion had taken for a large house was only the giant's glove. From this, you can see how huge the giant Skrymner must have been.

Skrymner showed himself to be a kind giant. He insisted upon carrying Thor's bag, putting it into his own wallet, and offered to take Thor and Loki to meet the King.

As they walked, the rising sun fell full upon the city of Utgard, the town of giants, whose huge brass gates glittered in the sunlight. Even though they were so far away, Thor could see how high they were – they made him and his companion seem no larger than grasshoppers.

Thor's Adventures among the Giants

Thor walked on and made his way to the palace. There, he asked to see the King.

After some time Thor was brought before Utgarda Loke, the King of the country. The King had never seen such small men before and there was something so funny in the sight that he burst out laughing.

"Though we are small compared with the giants," said Thor angrily, "we have powers that may surprise you."

"Really!" answered Utgarda Loke, raising his eyebrows. "What can you do?"

"I can drink a wine cup down be it never too big," replied the god.

And then a drinking horn was presented to Thor.

"If you are as great as you pretend to be," said the King, "you will drink it down in one go. Some people take two pulls at it, but the weakest among us can manage it in three."

Thor took up the horn and, being very thirsty, took a steady pull at it. He thought he had done very well but, on removing it from his lips, he was surprised to see how little had gone.

A second time he took a drink, but the horn was far from being emptied.

Again a third time he tried to finish it, but it was almost full to the brim.

"I am disappointed in you," said Utgarda Loke. "You are not half the man I took you for. I see it is no use asking you to do warrior's feats. I must test you in a simpler way. You shall try to lift my cat from the ground."

And a large grey cat came leaping along and planted itself firmly before Thor, showing its sharp claws.

Thor seized it, but in spite of all his efforts he was only able to raise one of the cat's paws from the ground.

"Huh!" exclaimed Utgarda Loke, "You are just a baby, fit only for the nursery. I believe that my old nurse, Hela, would be more than a match for you. Hela, come and wrestle with the mighty god Thor."

Out came an old woman. Her eyes were sunken, her arms and legs were thin, and her hair was white as snow.

She came towards Thor and tried to throw him to the ground. Though he put forth his whole strength into the contest, Thor was surprised to find how powerful she was. It needed all his efforts to keep on his feet. For a long time he was successful, but in the end Hela brought him down upon one knee, and Thor had to admit he was conquered.

Thor's Adventures among the Giants

Ashamed, he and Loki were making ready to leave the city quietly, when Utgarda Loke sent for them.

He made them a splendid feast and then went with them beyond the city gates.

"Now tell me honestly," said he to Thor, "what do you think of your success?"

"I am astounded and ashamed to be so beaten," replied the god.

"Ha! Ha!" laughed Utgarda Loke. "I knew that you were. However, as we are well out of the city I don't mind telling you a secret or two. The end of the drinking horn, though you did not see it, reached the sea. As fast as you emptied it, it filled again, so that you never could have drained it dry. But the next time that you stand upon the seashore, you will see how much less ocean there is after your large drinking.

"The grey cat was no cat, but the great Serpent of Midgard that twines round the world, and you lifted him so high that we were all quite frightened.

"But your last feat was the most wonderful of all, for Hela was none other than Death. Never did I see anyone before over whom Death had so little power.

"And now, my friend, go on your way and don't come near my city again, for I tell you plainly, I do not want you there. I shall use all kinds of enchantment to keep you out of it."

As he ended his speech, Thor raised his hammer, but Utgarda Loke had vanished.

"I will return to the city," said Thor.

But the giant city was nowhere to be

seen. A pasture spread itself out around him.

So Thor and his companion, thinking about their wonderful adventures, turned their steps towards home.

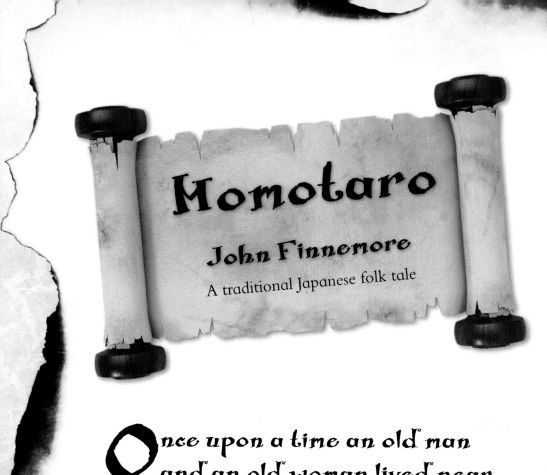

Momotaro

John Finnemore

A traditional Japanese folk tale

Once upon a time an old man and an old woman lived near a river at the foot of a mountain. Everyday the old man went to the mountain to cut wood and carry it home, while the old woman went to the river to wash clothes.

Now, the old woman was very unhappy because she had no children. It seemed to her that if she only had a son or a daughter she would be the most fortunate old woman in the world.

One day she was washing the clothes in the river, when she saw something floating down the stream towards her. It was a great peach, and she seized it and carried it home.

As she carried it she heard a sound like the cry of a child. She looked right and left, up and down, but no child was to be seen. She heard the cry again, and now she thought that it came from the big peach. So she cut the peach open at once and, to her great surprise and delight, she found that there was a baby sitting in the middle of it.

She took the child and brought him up, and because he was born in a peach she called him Momotaro, which means 'son of a peach'.

Momotaro grew up a strong, fine boy, and when he was seventeen years old he went out to seek his fortune. He had made up his mind to attack an island where a dreadful ogre lived.

The old woman gave Momotaro plenty of food to eat on the way — corn and rice wrapped in a bamboo leaf, and many other things — and away he went. He had not gone far when he met a wasp.

"Give me a share of your food, Momotaro," said the wasp, "and I will go with you and help you to overcome the dreadful ogre."

Momotaro

"With all my heart," said Momotaro, and he shared his food at once with the wasp.

Soon he met a crab, and the same agreement was made, and then with a chestnut, and last of all with a millstone.

So now the five companions journeyed on together towards the island of the ogre. When they reached the island they crept up to the house of the ogre and found that he was not in his room. So they soon made a plan to take advantage of his absence.

The chestnut laid itself down in the ash of a charcoal fire that had been burning on the hearth, the crab hid himself in a washing pan nearly full of water, the wasp settled in a dusky corner, the millstone climbed onto the roof, and Momotaro hid himself outside.

GRUESOME GIANTS AND AWFUL OGRES

Before long the ogre came back, and he went to the fire to warm his hands. The chestnut quickly cracked in the hot ashes and threw burning cinders over the ogre's hands. The ogre at once ran to the washing pan, and thrust his hands into it to cool them. The crab caught his fingers and pinched them till the ogre roared with pain. Snatching his hands out of the pan, the ogre leapt into the dusky corner as a safe place. But the wasp came and met him and stung him dreadfully.

In great fright and

misery, the ogre tried to run out of the room, but down came the millstone with a crash on his head and killed him at once.

So, without any trouble to himself, and with the help of his faithful friends, which he had made through his kindness, Momotaro got all the ogre's gold and his fortune was made.

Thirteenth

Thomas Frederick Crane

There was once a father who had thirteen sons, the youngest of whom was named Thirteenth. The father had hard work to support his children, but he made what little money he could gathering herbs.

One day, the King sent out a notice in the city that the person who would go and steal the ogre's bed covering would receive

Thirteenth

a reward of gold. Thirteenth's brothers went
to the King and said, "Majesty, we have a
brother named Thirteenth, who is bold
enough to do that and other things too."

The king said, "Bring him to me at once."

They brought Thirteenth, who said,
"Majesty, how is it possible to steal the ogre's
bed covering? If he sees me he will eat me!"

"No matter, you must go," said the King.
"I know that you are bold."

So Thirteenth went to the house of the
ogre, who was away. The ogress was in the
kitchen. Thirteenth entered quietly and hid
himself under the bed. At night, the ogre
returned. He ate his supper and went to bed,
saying as he did so, "I smell the smell of
human flesh. When I see it, I will eat it!"

The ogress replied, "Be still, no one has

entered here." The ogre began to snore, and
Thirteenth pulled the bed covering a little.
But the ogre woke up and called out,
"What is that?" Thirteenth began to mew
like a cat. The ogress said, "Scat! Scat!" and
clapped her hands. She then fell asleep
again with the ogre. Thirteenth gave a hard
pull, seized the bed covering and ran away.

The King was so pleased with the bed
covering that he issued another notice: he
would give a measure of gold to whoever
brought him the ogre's pillow. Thirteenth
said, "Majesty, how is that possible? The
pillow is full of little bells, and you must
know that the ogre awakens at the
slightest breath."

"I know nothing about it," said the
king. "I just want to have the pillow."

Thirteenth

So Thirteenth departed, and went and crept under the ogre's bed. At midnight he stretched out his hand very softly, but the little bells all sounded.

"What is that?" said the ogre.

"Nothing," replied the ogress, "perhaps it is the wind that makes them ring." But the ogre, who was suspicious, pretended to sleep, but kept his ears open. Thirteenth stretched out his hand again. Alas! The ogre put out his arm and seized him.

"Now you are caught! Just wait, I will have you for my supper." Then he put Thirteenth in a barrel. The ogre began to feed him on raisins and figs to get him fat enough to make a fine feast for him and his wife.

After a time, the ogre said, "Stick out your finger, little Thirteenth, so that I can see whether you are fat." Thirteenth saw a mouse's tail and stuck that out.

"Ah, how thin you are!" said the ogre. "And besides, you don't smell good! Eat, my son. Take the raisins and figs, and get fat soon!" After some days the ogre told him again to put out his finger and Thirteenth stuck out a splinter of wood. "Eh, wretch! Are you still so skinny? Eat, eat, and get fat soon."

Thirteenth

At the end of the month, Thirteenth had nothing more to stick out, and had to show his finger. The ogre cried out in joy, "He is fat, he is fat! Quick, my ogress, heat the oven for three nights and three days, for I am going to invite our relatives, and we will make a fine banquet of Thirteenth."

The ogress heated the oven for three days and three nights. Then she let Thirteenth out of the barrel, and said to him, "Come here, Thirteenth. You are going to help me put the lamb in the oven." But Thirteenth knew what she was planning, and when he approached the oven he said, "Ah, mother ogress, what is that black thing in the corner of the oven?" The ogress stooped down a little but saw nothing.

"Stoop down again," said Thirteenth, "so

293

that you can see it." When the ogress stooped down again, Thirteenth seized her by the feet and threw her into the oven. He then closed the oven door and ran home.

After this, the King said to Thirteenth, "Listen, Thirteenth. To complete your brave tasks, I want you to bring me the ogre himself, in person, alive and well."

"How can I, Your Majesty?" said Thirteenth. But he thought awhile, then added, "I will have a try."

Thirteenth had a strong chest made, and disguised himself with a long, false beard. He went to the ogre's house and called out to him, "Do you know Thirteenth? The wretch! He has killed some of my brothers, but I'll catch him! And when I catch him, I will shut him up in this chest!"

At these words the ogre drew near and said, "I, too, would like to help you, for you don't know what he has done to me." And he began to tell his story.

The pretending old man said, "I do not know Thirteenth. Do you know him?"

"Yes, sir."

"Then tell me, how tall is he?"

"As tall as I am."

"If that is so," said Thirteenth, "let us see whether this chest will hold him. If it will hold you, it will hold him."

"Oh, good idea!" said the ogre, and he got into the chest. Then Thirteenth shut the chest and nailed it up, put it on a cart and went back to the city.

When he arrived, the King had an iron chain attached to the ogre's hands and feet, and made him gnaw bones for the rest of his miserable life. The King gave Thirteenth a huge pile of riches and treasures, and asked him always to stay by his side.

The Giant of the Flood

Gertrude Landa

Just before the world was drowned, all the animals gathered in front of the Ark and Father Noah carefully inspected them.

Then the various creatures began to march forwards into the Ark. Father Noah watched them closely. Something seemed to be troubling him.

"I wonder," he said, "how I can get a

unicorn, and how I shall get it into the Ark."

"I can bring you a unicorn," said a voice of thunder. Turning round, Noah saw the giant, Og. "But you must agree to save me, too, from the flood."

"Go away," cried Noah. "You are a demon, not a human being. I can have no dealings with you."

"Pity me," whined the giant. "Look how my figure is shrinking and shrinking. Once I was so tall that I could drink water from the clouds and toast fish at the sun. I'm not afraid that I shall be drowned, but that all the food will be destroyed and that I shall die of hunger."

Noah, however, only smiled. But he grew serious again when Og brought a unicorn. It was as big as a mountain,

The Giant of the Flood

although the giant said that it was the smallest he could find.

For some time Noah was puzzled about what to do, but at last a bright idea struck him. He attached the huge unicorn to the Ark by a rope fastened to its horn, so that it could swim alongside and be fed.

Og seated himself on a mountain near at hand and watched the rain pouring down. Faster and faster it fell until the rivers overflowed and the waters began to rise rapidly on the land and sweep all things away.

Father Noah stood gloomily before the door of the Ark until the water reached his neck. Then it swept him inside. The door closed with a bang, and the Ark rose on the flood and began to move along. The

unicorn swam alongside, and as it passed
Og, the giant jumped on to its back!

"See, Father Noah," he cried, with a huge
chuckle, "you will have to save me after all.
I will snatch all the food you put through

The Giant of the Flood

the window for the unicorn."

Noah saw that it was useless to argue with Og, who might sink the Ark with his tremendous strength.

"I will make a bargain with you," Noah shouted from a window. "I will feed you, but you must promise to be a servant to my descendants."

Og was very hungry, so he accepted the conditions and devoured his first breakfast.

The rain continued to fall in great big sheets that shut out the light of day. However, inside the Ark all was bright and cheerful. Some of the animals were troublesome and Noah got no sleep at all. The lion had a bad attack of fever.

One day the rain stopped, the clouds rolled away and the sun shone brilliantly again. How strange the world looked! It was like a vast ocean. Nothing but water could be seen anywhere, and only one or two of the highest mountain tops peeped above the flood. All the world was drowned, and Noah gazed on the scene from one of the windows with tears in his eyes. Og, riding on the unicorn behind the Ark, was quite happy.

"Ha, ha!" he laughed. "I shall be able to eat and drink just as much as I like now and shall never be troubled by those tiny little creatures, the mortals."

"Be not so sure," said Noah. "Those tiny men and women shall be your masters and shall outlive you and the whole race of giants and demons."

The giant did not like that idea. He knew

that whatever Noah said would come true.
He was so sad that he ate no food for two
days, and began to grow smaller and
thinner. Og became more and more
unhappy as, day by day, the water went
down and the mountains began to appear.
At last the Ark rested on Mount Ararat, and
Og's long ride came to an end.

"I will soon leave you, Father Noah," he
said. "I shall wander round the world to see
what is left of it."

"You cannot go until I permit you," said
Noah. "Have you forgotten our agreement
so soon? You must be my servant. I have
work for you."

Giants are not fond of work, and Og,
who was the father of all the giants, was
lazy. He only wanted to eat and sleep, but

he knew he was in Noah's power, and he cried when he saw the land appear again.

"Stop," commanded Noah. "Do you want to drown the world all over again with your big tears?"

So Og sat on a mountain and rocked from side to side, crying silently to himself. He watched the animals leave the Ark and had to do all the hard work when Noah's children built houses. Daily he complained that he was shrinking to the size of a human, for Noah said there was not too much food.

One day Noah said to him, "Come with me, Og. I am going around the world to plant fruit and flowers to make the earth beautiful. I need your help."

For many days they wandered all over

the earth, and Og had to carry the heavy bag of seeds. The last thing Noah planted was the grapevine.

"What is this – food or drink?" asked Og.

"Both," replied Noah. "It can be eaten or its juice made into wine." As he planted it, he blessed the grape. "You shall be," he said, "a plant pleasing to the eye. Bear fruit that will be food for the hungry and a cheering drink to the thirsty."

Og himself often drank too much and many years afterward, when he was a servant to the patriarch Abraham, he was scolded until he became so frightened that one of his teeth dropped out. Abraham made an ivory chair for himself from this tooth. Afterwards Og became King of Bashan, but he forgot his agreement with

Noah. Instead of helping men, Og came to attack them. "I will kill them all with one blow," he declared.

Using all his enormous strength Og uprooted a mountain and, raising it high above his head, prepared to drop it on the people and crush them.

But a wonderful thing happened. The mountain was full of grasshoppers and ants who had bored millions of tiny holes in it. When King Og raised the great mass, it crumbled in his hands and fell over his head and round his neck like a collar. He tried to pull it off, but his teeth became tangled in the mass. As he danced about in rage and pain, Moses, the leader of the Israelites, approached him.

Moses was a tiny man compared with Og. With a mighty effort Moses jumped ten feet into the air and, raising his sword, he managed to strike the giant on the ankle and wound him.

And so, after many years, the terrible giant of the flood died because he broke his word to Father Noah.

WEIRD AND WONDERFUL BEASTS

John Malin and the Bull-man

Katharine Pyle

A Louisiana tale

John Malin worked as a servant for a fine lady. The lady had a friend who was a handsome man with a fine, deep voice. The gentleman's name was Mr Bulbul. He often came to the house to take meals with the lady and he always spoke to John Malin very pleasantly. But John could not bear him.

Now, not far from the lady's house there

was a pasture, and in this pasture was a bull – a fine, handsome animal. John Malin often saw it there.

After a while, John began to notice that whenever Mr Bulbul came to the house, which was almost every day, the bull disappeared from the pasture. And whenever the bull was in the pasture, there was nothing to be seen of the gentleman.

"That is a curious thing," said John to himself. "I will watch and find out what this means. I am sure something is wrong."

So one day, John went out and hid himself behind some rocks at the edge of the pasture. The bull was grazing with its head down and did not see John. After a while the bull raised its head and looked all about to see if there was anyone around.

WEIRD AND WONDERFUL BEASTS

John Malin and the Bull-man

Then it dropped on its knees and cried, "Beau Madjam, fat Madjam, djam, djam, djara, djara!"

All of a sudden, the bull turned into a man. The man was Mr Bulbul, who came to visit John's mistress.

John Malin ran home to his mistress and said, "Dear Mistress, Mr Bulbul is not a man at all, but a bull monster. He uses magic to make himself look like a man so as to come to see you."

The lady began to laugh. "You are either crazy or dreaming," she said. But John Malin insisted that what he told her was true. "I have seen it and I know it," he said. "I will prove it to you."

After that, John went away by himself and thought and thought. He tried to remember the exact words the bull had said when he turned himself into a man, but he could not be sure what they were.

So the next day, John went out and hid himself behind the rocks again, taking care, as before, that the bull should not see him. The bull's head was down and it was eating grass.

However, it soon raised its head and looked all about. Seeing no one, the creature dropped on its knees and bellowed, "Beau Madjam, fat Madjam, djam, djam, djara, djara!"

All of a sudden, the bull became a man and walked away in the direction of the lady's house.

John Malin followed Mr Bulbul, saying over and over to himself quietly, "Beau

John Malin and the Bull-man

Madjam, fat Madjam, djam, djam, djara, djara. Beau Madjam, fat Madjam, djam, djam, djara, djara!"

When John Malin reached the house, Mr Bulbul was in the salon with his mistress. John could hear them talking together.

John Malin took a tray of cakes and wine and carried it into the salon, just as though his mistress had ordered him to do so. He went over to Mr Bulbul, so he was close in front of him, and then he said in a very low voice, as though just to himself, "Beau Madjam, fat Madjam, djam, djam, djara, djara!"

Such a noise you never heard. The fine Mr Bulbul bellowed aloud and jumped up, smashing his chair. The lady shrieked and almost fainted. Then, right there before them, Mr Bulbul's head grew long and hairy, horns sprouted from his forehead, his arms turned into legs and his hands and feet into hoofs, and he became a bull.

He galloped across the salon in a fright, his hoofs clattering on the floor. The bull burst out through the glass door so fast that he carried it away on his horns and back into the pasture with him.

John Malin and the Bull-man

Then the lady knew that everything John Malin had told her was true and she could not thank him enough.

John Malin was very happy, but he was sure the bull would try to revenge itself on him in some way or other. At last, John grew so afraid that he decided to go and talk to a wise man he knew who dealt in magic. John told him everything that had happened, then said, "And now, I am afraid, for I think he means to harm me."

"You do well to be afraid," said the wise man. "Bulbul will certainly try to do you harm. He knows much magic, but my magic is stronger than his and I will help you. Get me three owl's eggs and a cup of black goat's milk and bring them here."

John Malin went away and got the three

owl's eggs and the cup of black goat's milk, though they were not easy to find. Then he brought them to the wise man.

The wise man took them from him. He rolled the owl's eggs in the milk and made magic over them. Then he gave them back to John. "Keep these by you all the time," he said. "Then if the bull comes after you do thus and so, and this and the other, and you will have no more trouble with him."

John Malin thanked the wise man, gave him a piece of silver and went away with the eggs tied up in his handkerchief.

He had not gone more than halfway home, and was just coming out from a wood, when he heard a loud noise and the bull burst out of the trees and came charging towards him.

John Malin and the Bull-man

Quick as a flash, John Malin put the eggs in his mouth and climbed up a tree. The eggs were not broken.

The bull galloped up and struck the tree with its horns. "You think you are safe, but I will soon have you down," it cried.

Then the bull changed into a man. He had an axe in his hands and began to chop down the tree. *Gip, gop! Gip, gop!* The chips flew and the branches trembled.

John tried to remember the words that would turn the man back into a bull, but he was so frightened he could not think of them. What he did remember were the eggs that the man had given him. He took one out of his mouth and dropped it down on the bull-man's right shoulder. At once the bull-man's right arm fell off and the axe dropped to the ground. However, this did not trouble the bull-man. He picked up the axe with his left hand and chopped away, *Gip, gop! Gip, gop!* The chips flew faster than ever.

Then John Malin dropped the second egg down on the bull-man's left shoulder and his left arm fell off. Now the bull-man had no arms, but he took up the axe in his mouth and went on chopping, *Gip, gop! Gip, gop!* The whole tree shook and trembled.

Then John Malin dropped the third

320

and last egg down on the bull-man's head and at once his head fell off.

That ended the bull-man's magic. He could do nothing more and had to turn into a bull again. Away he galloped, with his tail in the air, and that was the last John Malin ever saw of him. What became of him nobody ever knew, but he must have gone far, far away.

John Malin climbed down from the tree and went home. After that, he lived very happily in the lady's house and was like a son to her.

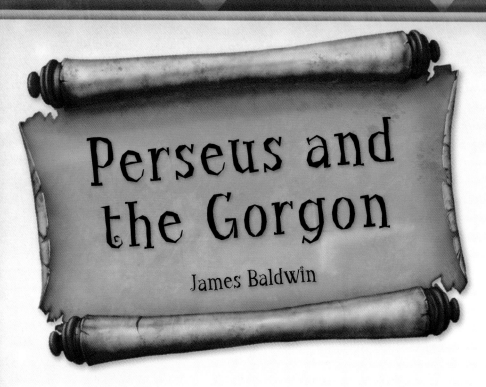

Perseus and the Gorgon

James Baldwin

*The Greek hero, Perseus, has been summoned
by his King, who has a task for him.*

"The Gorgons," said the King, "are
three terrible demon sisters who
live in the middle of Africa. Their bodies are
covered with dragon scales, their hands are
claws, they have snakes instead of hair, and
they have teeth as long as tusks. Whoever
looks upon them is turned to stone. All three

Perseus and the Gorgon

are dreadful, but the one who is named Medusa is the most dreadful of all. Now I have been thinking, as you are so fond of adventures, you will go and cut off Medusa's head."

Perseus was much too brave to refuse or even to think of refusing. So he lay down to get a little sleep before starting out.

He dreamt that Pluto, Minerva and Mercury came to his bedside and that each gave him a parting present. Pluto gave him a helmet, Minerva a shield and Mercury a pair of sandals, with little wings fastened to them. But the dream was not as strange as what he found when he woke up. There, on his bed, actually lay the helmet, the shield of polished steel and the winged sandals.

Well, somebody must have put them

there. So first Perseus put on the helmet, then he slung the shield over his shoulders, and last of all he put the winged sandals on his feet. When the wings spread themselves at his heels, and carried him high up into the air, he began to think that the visit from the gods must have been something more than a dream.

Perseus went up so high that the earth looked like a large map spread out below him. But not till nearly nightfall did he see, in the far distance, a cluster of palm trees. Reaching the palm trees at last, he found, in the midst of the cluster, a wooden hut.

He entered and found three very old women warming their hands at a few burning sticks. As he came in, the three crones turned their faces towards him.

Perseus and the Gorgon

Perseus saw that one of them had only one eye and no teeth, that another had only one tooth and no eye, and that the third had neither teeth nor eyes.

"I am a traveller," said Perseus, "and have lost my way. Will you kindly tell me where I am?"

"Come in and show yourself," said the crone who had the eye, sharply. "I must see who you are before I answer," she added, even though her one eye was looking straight at Perseus.

"Here I am," said Perseus, stepping into the middle of the room. "I suppose you can see me now."

"It's very strange – very strange!" said the old woman. "Sisters, I hear a man's voice but I see no man!"

"Nonsense, sister!" said the one who had the tooth. "You can't have put the eye in right. Let me try."

To the amazement of Perseus, the first old woman took out her eye and passed it to the second, who, after giving it a polish, put it into her own face and looked round. But she also saw nothing.

Perseus and the Gorgon

So they kept passing the eye round from one to another, and yet they could see nothing. At last Perseus, feeling terribly hot and tired, took off Pluto's helmet to cool himself, when suddenly –

"There he is! I see him now!" exclaimed the old woman who, at that moment, happened to be using the eye.

And so Perseus found out that his helmet made him invisible when he put it on.

He said, "Will you put me on the right road to where I want to go?"

It was the one who happened to have the eye in her head that always spoke.

"We are the three Grey Sisters. And where do you want to go?"

"I want to visit the Gorgons, particularly Medusa," said Perseus. "Do you happen to know where they are?"

"Of course we know! But never, no, never will we tell you where they live or the way to get there."

"Never!" croaked the old woman with the tooth.

"Never!" mumbled the third.

Perseus did all he could to persuade them, but they were so stubborn that he was only wasting words. Meanwhile, they laid out their supper, which they ate in a very strange way. They took turns with the one tooth that they had among them, and passed it round from one to the other, just as they did with their one eye. After supper, they put the eye and the tooth into a little box while they took a nap. Perseus, watching for his opportunity, snatched up the box, put on his helmet and cried out, "Now tell me the way to Medusa, or else you shall never see or eat again!"

The poor old Grey Sisters went down on their knees and begged him to give them back their only tooth and their only eye. But he said, "It is my turn to be stubborn. Tell me where to find Medusa."

"Very well," said the eldest Grey Sister, "you must go straight on, night and day, until you come into the country of King Atlas. Near the King's palace is a garden where the trees bear golden apples, guarded by a dragon. If the dragon does not devour you, you must pass the garden gate and go on, a long, long way, till you come to a great lake where, if you do not find the Gorgons, you will be a lucky man."

Weird and Wonderful Beasts

Perseus gave the old women back their tooth and eye, which they received with joy, left the hut and travelled on. After many days he came into a fertile country where he found a great garden enclosed by a high wall, and sure enough, at the gate sat a monstrous dragon with glaring eyes. But Perseus, wearing his invisible helmet, passed by safely.

In time he came to the lake, where he took off his helmet to quench his thirst. While he was drinking, Perseus was startled by the approach of what sounded like a mighty rush of wind. He had just enough time to put his helmet on again before he saw, reflected in the lake, the flying form of the terrible Medusa – the Gorgon – whom he had vowed to slay.

Perseus and the Gorgon

Medusa, not seeing Perseus, sat down beside him with folded wings.

Perseus remembered what would happen to him if he looked at Medusa. And yet how in the world was he to fight her without looking at her? Suddenly he thought of Minerva's shield, which was polished like a mirror. He turned it towards Medusa and saw not herself, but her reflection in the polished shield, which did just as well.

She was indeed a monster – even more terrible than Perseus had expected. Medusa was of gigantic size, hideous and cruel in face, with the scales and wings of a dragon, horrible claws, and hundreds of writhing and hissing snakes on her head instead of hair. No wonder that anyone who looked on her was turned into stone straight away.

Perseus, wearing his helmet and guiding himself by his mirror, from which he never moved his eyes, drew his blade and sprang upon the monster. He gave one stroke just between her chin and where her scales began, and, in a single moment, her hideous head was rolling on the sand. The snakes gave one last hiss, and the deed was done.

Still keeping his eyes turned away, Perseus, using his shield as a mirror, found Medusa's head. He slung it out of his sight behind him. Then, rising into the air, Perseus flew homewards.

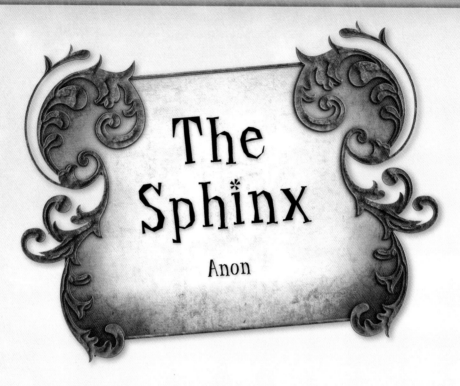

The Sphinx

Anon

Many, many years ago, there was a terrible monster that haunted the land of Egypt. It was called the Sphinx, and it caused terror to the lands around the city of Thebes. The Sphinx had the body of a strong, powerful lion, with sharp claws covered in dried blood. Its head was that of a woman – not a gentle, smiling woman, but a terrible, cruel-faced woman.

334

The Sphinx

She lurked on the road into the town of Thebes, and all travellers had to pass her to continue along the road. For on one side there was a high cliff that no one could climb, and on the other a terrible precipice that fell down, down, down to a rocky river far below. Every time a traveller passed the Sphinx, she caught them, and told them that she would only let them go if they could answer her question.

"What animal is it that goes on four feet in the morning, on two feet at noon, and on three legs in the evening?" the Sphinx would ask, and her lips would curve in a smile.

No one could answer the question and she would throw them over the precipice. There wasn't anyone that could defeat her because no one could guess the riddle.

WEIRD AND WONDERFUL BEASTS

The Sphinx

One day, the Greek Oedipus came travelling towards the city of Thebes. The Sphinx crouched face to face with him and spoke the riddle that none had been able to guess.

"What animal is it that in the morning goes on four feet, at noon on two feet, and in the evening on three legs?"

Oedipus, hiding his dread of the terrible creature, sat on the sand and thought carefully. Then he answered, "Man. In childhood he crawls on hands and knees, as a grown-up he walks upright on two legs, but in old age he needs a stick to help him."

At this reply the Sphinx uttered a cry, sprang from the rock into the valley below, and died where she had thrown so many people before her. Oedipus had guessed the answer correctly.

When Oedipus came to the city and told the people of Thebes that the Sphinx was gone, they greeted him as their rescuer. They took Oedipus to the best house in the town and begged him to rest while they washed his feet and combed his hair. Then they brought a feast of cheese, tender young lamb, grapes, bread and honey, with tall jugs of red wine. They invited Oedipus to rest, eat and drink while they sang songs in his praise. The evil monster would trouble them no more and they could walk their roads in peace at last.

The Bogey-Beast

Flora Annie Steel

There was once a woman who was very cheerful, though she had little to make her so. She was poor and lonely. The woman lived in a little cottage and earned a small living by running errands for her neighbours, getting a bite here and a sup there, as reward for her services. She always looked as lively and cheery as if she had not a want in the world.

The Bogey-Beast

Now, one summer evening, as the woman was walking along the high road to her cottage, full of smiles as ever, she saw a big black pot lying in the ditch.

"Goodness me!" she cried, "That would be just the very thing for me if I only had something to put in it. But I haven't. Now who could have left it in the ditch?"

She looked about her expecting the owner would not be far off, but she could see nobody.

"Maybe there is a hole in it," she went on, "and that's why it has been cast away. But it would do fine to put a flower in for my window, so I'll take it home with me."

And with that she lifted the lid and looked inside. "Mercy me!" she cried. "If it isn't full of gold pieces. Here's luck!"

Weird and Wonderful Beasts

And so it was, full of great gold coins. Well, at first the woman simply stood still, wondering if she was standing on her head or her heels. Then she began saying to herself, "Crikey! But I do feel rich. I feel awfully rich!"

After she had said this many times, she began to wonder how she was going to get her treasure home. It was too heavy for her to carry. She could see no better way than to tie the end of her shawl to the pot and drag it behind her.

"It will soon be dark," she said to herself as she walked along. "So much the better! The neighbours will not see what I'm bringing home. I shall have all night to myself and will be able to think about what to do! Maybe I'll buy a grand house and just sit by the fire with a cup of tea and do no work at all like a queen. Or maybe I'll bury it at the bottom of the garden and just keep a bit in the old china teapot. Or maybe – Goody! Goody! I feel that grand I don't know myself!"

By this time she was a bit tired of dragging such a heavy weight and, stopping to rest a while, she turned to look at the treasure behind her.

It wasn't a pot of gold at all! It was nothing but a lump of silver.

The woman stared at it, rubbed her eyes and stared at it again. "Well! I never!" she said at last. "And me thinking it was a pot of gold! I must have been dreaming. But this is luck! Silver is far less trouble – easier to mind and not so easily stolen. Those gold pieces would have been the death of me, and with this great lump of silver – "

So she went off again, planning what she would do and feeling very rich. Becoming a bit tired again, she stopped to rest and looked around to see if her treasure was safe. But she saw nothing but a great lump of iron!

"Well! I never!" she said again. "And I mistook it for silver! I must have been dreaming. But this is luck! It's really convenient. I can get penny pieces for old iron, and penny pieces are a great deal handier for me than gold and silver. Why! I should never have slept a wink for fear of being robbed. But a penny piece comes in useful, and I shall sell that iron for a lot and be rich – rolling rich."

The Bogey-Beast

So on she walked, full of plans as to how she would spend her penny pieces. Once more she stopped to rest and looked round to see if her treasure was safe. And this time she saw nothing but a big stone!

"Well! I never!" she cried, full of smiles. "And to think I mistook it for iron. I must have been dreaming. But here's luck indeed, with me badly wanting a stone to stick open the gate. It's a change for the better! It's a fine thing to have good luck."

So, all in a hurry to see how the stone would keep the gate open, the woman walked off down the hill till she came to her own cottage. She unlatched the gate and then turned to unfasten her shawl from the stone, which lay on the path behind her. It was a stone sure enough. There was plenty of light to see it lying there, sweet and peaceful as a stone should.

So the woman bent over the stone to unfasten the shawl end, when –

"Oh my!"

All of a sudden the stone gave a jump, a squeal, and in one moment it was as big as a haystack. Then it let down four great, lanky legs and threw out two long ears, flourished a great long tail, and romped off, kicking and squealing and whinnying and laughing like a naughty, mischievous boy!

The woman stared after the creature till it was nearly out of sight, and then she burst out laughing.

"Well!" she chuckled, "I am in luck! Quite the luckiest body hereabouts. Fancy my seeing the Bogey-Beast all to myself!"

The Bogey-Beast

And making myself so free with it too! My goodness! I do feel uplifted – that grand!"

So she went into her cottage and spent the evening chuckling over her good luck.

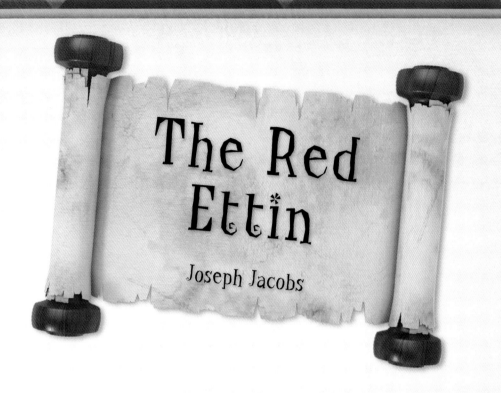

The Red Ettin*

Joseph Jacobs

There was once a widow who lived on a small bit of ground, which she rented from a farmer. She had two sons, and it was time for the widow to send them away to seek their fortunes.

So the oldest young man went to seek his fortune first. And he went all that day and all the next day. On the third day, in the afternoon, he came up to where a shepherd was sitting with a flock of sheep. He went up to the shepherd and asked him who the sheep belonged to. The shepherd answered, "The Red Ettin of Ireland."

The shepherd also told the young man to beware of the beasts he should meet next, for they were of a very different kind from any he had yet seen.

So the young man went on, and he saw very dreadful beasts with two heads, and on every head four horns. He was frightened and ran away from them as fast as he could.

The young man was glad when he came to a castle that stood on a small hill, with the door standing wide open to the wall. He went into the castle for shelter, and saw an old woman sitting beside the kitchen fire.

The Red Ettin

He asked her if he might stay for the night, as he was tired from a long journey. The old woman said he might, but that the castle was not a good place for him to be in. It belonged to the Red Ettin, a terrible beast with three heads, who spared no living man it could get hold of.

The young man would have gone away, but he was afraid of the beasts outside of the castle. He begged the old woman to hide him as best she could, and not tell the Red Ettin he was there. He thought if he could last the night, he might get away in the morning without meeting with the beasts, and so escape.

But he had not been long in his hiding place before the awful Red Ettin came in. And no sooner was he in, than he cried out:

"Snouk but and snouk ben,

   I find the smell of an earthly man.

   Be he living, or be he dead,

   His heart this night shall kitchen

     my bread."

The monster soon found the poor young man and pulled him from his hole. He then told him that if he could answer three questions, his life would be spared.

So the first of the Red Ettin's heads asked, "A thing without an end, what's that?" But the young man knew not. Then the second head said, "The smaller, the more dangerous, what's that?" But the young man knew not. And then the third head asked, "When does the dead carry the living, riddle me that?" But the young man knew not and had to give up.

The Red Ettin

He was unable to answer one of these questions, and the Red Ettin took a mallet and knocked him on the head, and turned him into a pillar of stone.

The morning after, the younger brother told his mother that the time had now come for him to go upon his travels also. After he had travelled far, he met with an old woman who asked him if he would give her a bit of his bread. He said, "I will gladly do that." For the bread she gave him a magical wand that might be of service to him, if he took care to use it rightly.

He went on a great way farther, and then he came to the shepherd. When he asked whose sheep they were, the answer was, "The Red Ettin of Ireland."

When he came to the place where the

monstrous beasts were standing, he did not stop nor run away, but went boldly through them. One came up, roaring with an open mouth to devour him, but when he struck it with his wand, it was in an instant dead at his feet.

He soon came to the Red Ettin's castle, where he knocked and was admitted. The old woman by the fire warned the young man of the terrible Red Ettin, and what had been the fate of his brother. But he was not to be daunted. The monster soon came in, saying:

"Snouk but and snouk ben,
  I find the smell of an earthly man.
  Be he living, or be he dead,
  His heart shall be kitchen to
    my bread."

He quickly caught sight of the young
man and bade him come forth on the floor.
And then he put the three questions to him.
But the young man had been told
everything by the good fairy, so he was able
to answer all the questions.

When the first head asked, "What's a
thing without an end?" he said, "A bowl."
And when the second head said, "The
smaller, the more dangerous, what's that?"
he said at once, "A bridge." And last, the
third head said, "When does the dead carry
the living, riddle me that?" The young man
answered at once and said, "When a ship
sails on the sea with men inside her." When
the Red Ettin heard this, he knew that his
power was gone. The young man took up
an axe and cut off the monster's three heads.

The Red Ettin

The old woman took him upstairs and opened a great many doors. Out of every door came a beautiful lady who had been imprisoned there by the Red Ettin, and one of the ladies was the King's daughter. The old woman took the young man down into a low room, and there stood a stone pillar. He pointed his wand at it and his brother started to life.

All the prisoners were overjoyed at their rescue, for which they thanked the young man. The next day they all set out for the King's court. The King married his daughter to the young man who had rescued her and gave a noble's daughter to his brother. And so they all lived happily for the rest of their days.

The Master and his Pupil

Joseph Jacobs

There was once a very clever man in the north country who knew all the languages under the sun. He had one big book bound in black calf skin and clasped with iron, and with iron corners. It was chained to a table, which was fastened to the floor. When he read out of this book, he unlocked it with an iron key, and no one but he read from it, for it contained all the secrets of the world. It told how many angels there were in heaven. And it told of the demons, how many of them there were, what their powers and names were, and how they might be summoned and chained to be slaves to man.

The master had a pupil who was a foolish lad. He was never allowed to look into the black book or to enter the private room.

One day, when the master was out, the lad, as curious as could be, hurried to the private room. This was where his master kept his equipment for changing copper into gold and lead into silver. And where was his mirror, in which he could see all that was passing in the world. And where was the shell, which, when held to the ear, whispered all the words that were being spoken by anyone the master wanted to know about.

The lad tried in vain to turn copper and lead into gold and silver. He looked long into the mirror – smoke and clouds passed over it, but he saw nothing clear. And the shell to his ear produced only indistinct murmurings, like the breaking of distant seas on an unknown shore. "I can do nothing," he said, "as I don't know the right words to utter, and they are locked up in the magic book."

He looked round and saw the book was unfastened – the master had forgotten to lock it before he went out. The lad rushed to it and opened the book. It was written with red and black ink, and much of it he could not understand. But he put his finger on a line and read it through.

At once the room became dark and the house trembled. A clap of thunder rolled through the passage and the old room. And there stood before the lad a horrible monster, breathing fire and with eyes like burning lamps. It was the demon Beelzebub, whom he had called up to serve him.

"Set me a task!" said he, with a voice like the roaring of an iron furnace.

The lad only trembled and his hair stood up on his head.

"Set me a task!"

But the lad could not speak. Then the monster stepped towards him and, putting forth his hands, touched the lad's throat. The fingers burned his flesh. "Set me a task!"

"Water the flower!" cried the lad in

The Master and his Pupil

despair, pointing to a geranium that stood in a pot on the floor. Instantly the monster left the room, but in another instant he returned with a barrel on his back. He poured its contents over the flower. And again and again he went and came, pouring more and more water, till it was ankle-deep on the floor of the room.

"Enough, enough!" gasped the lad. But the monster took no notice. The lad didn't know the words by which to send him away, and still he fetched water.

It rose to the lad's knees and still more water was poured. It rose to his waist, and Beelzebub still kept on bringing barrels full. It rose to his armpits and he scrambled on top of the table. And now the water in the room stood up to the window and washed against the glass, and swirled around the lad's feet on the table. It still rose – it reached his chest. In vain he cried, but the monster would not be dismissed.

To this day, Beelzebub would have been pouring water, and would have drowned all Yorkshire. But the master remembered on his journey that he had not locked his book and came back. At the moment when the water was bubbling about the pupil's chin, the master rushed into the room and spoke the words that cast Beelzebub back into his fiery home.

And the master never left his book unlocked again.

The Cattle of Geryon

R E Francillon
From *Of Gods and Monsters*

The great Greek hero, Hercules, has been set a series of tasks by his cousin, King Eurystheus. Every time Eurystheus comes up with a task that he thinks is impossible, Hercules manages to complete it.

Eurystheus was at his wits' end coming up with work for his cousin. 'I must send Hercules to the very end of the earth,' thought Eurystheus. So he talked with every traveller who came to Mycenae, and in

The Cattle of Geryon

time had the good luck to hear of a suitable monster named Geryon, who lived in a cave at Gades, on the coast of Spain. This was very near indeed to what the Greeks then thought to be the end of the world.

Geryon, so the travellers reported, had three bodies and three heads, and kept large and valuable flocks and herds. 'That will be just the thing for Hercules!' thought Eurystheus. So he called Hercules and said, "Go to Gades and get me the cattle and the sheep of Geryon."

So Hercules set off for Spain by way of Egypt and the great Libyan desert.

He travelled on until one day he reached a pile of human skulls, nearly as big as a mountain. While wondering at the sight, a shadow fell over him and a big voice said,

WEIRD AND WONDERFUL BEASTS

"Yes, you may well look at that!
I have nearly enough now."

It was a giant, nearly as
high as the pile of skulls.
"And who are you?"
asked Hercules, "And
what are these?"

"I am Antaeus,"
answered the giant, "the
Sea is my father and the
Earth is my mother. I
am collecting skulls
in order to build a
temple with them,
upon my mother the Earth,
to my father the Sea."

"And how," asked Hercules, "have you
managed to get so many?"

The Cattle of Geryon

"By killing everybody I see and adding his skull to the heap – as I am going to add yours."

So saying, he seized Hercules to kill him. But he was amazed to find that he himself was dashed to the ground, with force enough to break any ordinary bones. However, Antaeus, though astonished, was not in the least hurt, so it was the turn of Hercules to be surprised. Again they grabbed at each other, and again Hercules threw the giant, with still greater strength. Again and again Hercules threw him, but

every time with greater difficulty. The more
he was thrown, the stronger the giant
became – he rose from every fall fresher
than before. If this went on, Antaeus would
become stronger than Hercules and would
end by winning.

Now, Hercules thought it seemed very
strange that each time the giant was dashed
to the ground, the fresher and stronger he
should grow.

'I see!' thought Hercules to himself. 'This
giant is the son of the Earth, so whenever
he falls, he is falling upon his own mother,
who strengthens and refreshes her son. I
must find another way.'

So thinking, Hercules put out all his
strength and lifted Antaeus in his arms. But
this time he did not dash him to the Earth –

he held him in the air and crushed him to death between his hands.

After this, Hercules travelled on without further adventure, until he reached the far western end of the Mediterranean Sea, which was thought to be the end of the world. It is where the south of Spain nearly touches Africa.

To get from there to Gades was no great distance. And to kill the monster Geryon, and to seize his flocks and herds for Eurystheus, was not very hard after what he had already done. But to drive such a number of sheep and cattle all the way from Gades in Spain to Mycenae in Greece was not an easy matter.

There was only one way of doing so without being stopped somewhere along the way by the sea, and this was by crossing two great mountain ranges – the Pyrenees and the Alps.

For one man to drive thousands of sheep and thousands of horned cattle over such mountains as those was the most tiresome and troublesome labour that Hercules had ever undergone.

He got as far as Italy without the loss of a single sheep or cow, and thought that he had seen the end of his trouble.

However, one morning, having counted the sheep and cattle as usual, and having gone some miles upon his day's journey, Hercules became aware that there was something wrong.

The sheep began to bleat and the cattle to bellow in an odd and excited way. And frequently, from behind him, Hercules heard an answering sound that at first he took for an echo. But no, it could not be that, for an echo would have repeated the bleating as well as the bellowing. And what Hercules heard behind him was the sound of bellowing only – precisely like that of Geryon's cows.

Hercules counted the flocks and herds over again and, though he was convinced that it was all right at the start, he found a full dozen missing.

Now a dozen was not much to lose out of thousands. But Hercules had been ordered to bring back all of the herds and flocks, and he would have felt that he had not done his duty if he lost even one lamb on the way.

So, following the distant sound, Hercules drove his sheep and cattle back across the hills, league after league, till he reached a huge, black cavern, the mouth of which was heaped with human bones.

His cattle became more excited and more difficult to control, for the sound Hercules was following came from within this huge cave.

Hercules was about to enter the cave and search it, when a three-headed ogre came out. The ogre's three mouths, when he opened them to speak, breathed smoke and flames.

"This is my cave," said he, with all three mouths at once, "and no man shall enter it but I."

"I only want my cattle," said Hercules.

The Cattle of Geryon

"Bring them out to me."

"Cattle?" asked the ogre. "There are no cattle here. I swear it by the head of my own mother."

"And who was she," asked Hercules, "that her head is an oath to swear by?"

"I am Cacus, the son of the Gorgon Medusa," answered the ogre, "I swear—"

But before he could finish, there came such a bellowing from within the cave that the very cattle seemed as if they were saying that Cacus lied.

"I am sorry," said Hercules. "I am weary of travelling, and of monsters, and of giants, and of ogres, and of liars, and of thieves. I really do not want to kill anymore. You are not one of my labours and I have had enough trouble."

Cacus laughed. "Do you see those bones?" he asked. "They are all that is left of people who have looked for what they have lost in my cave."

"Then," said Hercules, "either you shall add mine to the heap or I will add yours."

The Cattle of Geryon

And presently the bones of Cacus the Robber were added to the heap and Hercules, having got his cattle back, at last reached Mycenae.

Talus, the Brass Giant

Charles Kingsley
From *The Heroes*

This is part of the story of Jason and the Argonauts. Jason and his warriors are travelling back to his home with the sorceress Medea, when they come to the island of Talus.

They rowed for many a weary day until their water was drunk and their food was eaten. But last they saw a long, steep island ahead.

"We will land here," they cried, "and fill our water casks upon the shore."

Talus, the Brass Giant

But when they came nearer to the island, they saw a wondrous sight. For on the cliffs stood a giant, taller than any mountain.

When the giant saw the ship Argo and her crew he came towards them, more swiftly than the swiftest horse, and he shouted to them, "You are pirates, you are robbers! If you land here, you shall die."

Then the heroes pulled on their oars in fear, but Medea spoke, "I know this giant. If strangers land, he leaps into his furnace, which flames there among the hills. And when he is red-hot, he rushes on them and burns them in his brass hands. But he has only one vein in all his body, filled with liquid fire, and this vein is closed with a nail. I will find out where the nail is placed, and when I have got it in my hands, you shall get water for your ship in peace."

So they took Medea and left
her alone on the shore. And
she stood there all alone in
her beauty, till the giant
strode back and was red-
hot from head to heel.

When the giant saw
the maiden he stopped.
Medea looked boldly up
into his face and sang a
magic song. Then she held up
a flash of crystal and said,

Talus, the Brass Giant

"I am Medea, the sorceress. My sister, Circe, gave me this and said, 'Go, reward Talus, the faithful giant, for his fame has gone out into all lands.' So I have come and I will pour this into your vein, so that you may live forever."

Talus listened to her false words and came near.

Medea said, "Dip yourself in the sea first to cool yourself, in case you burn my tender hands. Then show me the nail in your vein, and in that I will pour the liquid from the crystal flask."

Then Talus dipped himself, hissing, in the sea and then knelt before Medea and showed her the secret nail.

Medea drew the nail out gently, but she poured nothing in, and instead the liquid fire streamed forth.

Talus, the Brass Giant

Talus tried to leap up, crying, "You have betrayed me, false witch-maiden."

But Medea lifted up her hands before him and sang, till he sank beneath her spell.

And as Talus sank, the earth groaned beneath his weight and the liquid fire ran from his heel, like a stream of lava, down to the sea.

Then Medea laughed and called to the heroes, "Come and get water for your ship in peace."

So they came and found the giant lying dead. They fell down and kissed Medea's feet, watered their ship, took sheep and oxen, and so left that unfriendly shore.

And at last, after many weary days and nights, all worn and tired, the heroes saw once more their home, Iolcos, by the sea.

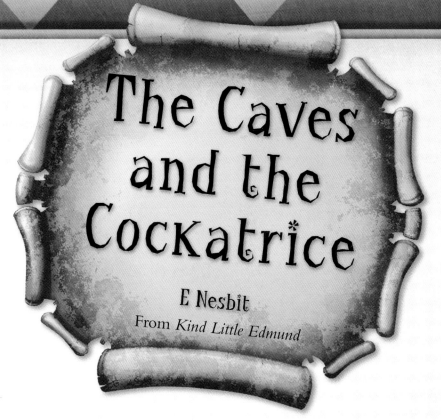

The Caves and the Cockatrice

E Nesbit
From *Kind Little Edmund*

Edmund was a boy. The people who did not like him said that he was the most tiresome boy that ever lived. But his grandmother and his friends said that he had an inquiring mind. His grandmother often added that he was the best of boys, but she was very kind and very old.

Edmund lived with his grandmother. She loved him very much, in spite of his inquiring mind, and hardly scolded him at all. Edmund went to school of course, now and then, and sometimes he could not prevent himself from learning something, but he never did it on purpose.

"It is such a waste of time," he said. "They only know what everybody knows. I want to find out new things that nobody has thought of but me."

"I don't think you're likely to find out anything that none of the wise men in the whole world have thought of all these thousands of years," said Granny.

Other boys played truant, of course, and they went blackberrying or wild plum gathering. But Edmund never went on the side of the town where the green woods and hedges grew. He always went up the mountain where the great rocks were, and where other people were afraid to go because of the strange noises that came out of the caves.

Edmund was not afraid of these noises, though they were very strange and terrible. He wanted to find out what made them.

One day, he did. He had invented, all by himself, a new kind of lantern made with a turnip and a tumbler. And when he added the candle out of Granny's candlestick, it gave quite a splendid light.

Edmund had to go to school the next day and he was caned – although he very straightforwardly explained that he had been too busy to have time to come to school the day before.

But the day after, Edmund got up and

took the lunch Granny had made for him
to take to school – two boiled eggs and an
apple turnover – and his lantern, and went
off to explore the caves.

The caves were very dark, but his lantern
lit them up beautifully. They were most
interesting, with stalactites and stalagmites
and fossils, and all the things you read
about. About halfway up the wall of the
cave, Edmund saw a hole. And, being a boy,
he climbed up to it and crept in. It was the
entrance to a rocky passage. "I am going to
find out something at last," said Edmund,
and on he went. The passage wound and
twisted, and twisted and turned, but
Edmund kept on going.

"My lantern's burning better and better,"
he said presently. But the next minute he

saw that all the light did not come from his lantern. It was a pale yellow light, and it shone down the passage through what looked like the chink of a door.

"I expect it's the fire in the middle of the earth," said Edmund.

But quite suddenly the fire ahead gave a pale flicker and went down.

The next moment, Edmund turned a corner and found himself in front of a rocky door. The door was ajar. He went in, and there was a round cave, like the dome of St Paul's. In the middle of the cave was a hole, like a very big washing basin, and in the middle of it Edmund saw a large, pale person sitting.

This person had a man's face, a griffin's body with big, feathery wings, a snake's tail,

WEIRD AND WONDERFUL BEASTS

and a cock's comb and neck feathers.

"Whatever are you?" said Edmund.

"I'm a poor, starving cockatrice," answered the pale person, "and I shall die – oh, I know I shall! My fire's gone out! I must have been asleep. I have to stir it seven times round with my tail once in a hundred years to keep it alight, and my watch must have been wrong. And now I shall die."

Now, Edmund was a kindhearted boy. "Cheer up," he said. "I'll light your fire for you." And off he went. In a few minutes he came back with a great armful of sticks from the pine trees outside. And with these, and a lesson book or two that he had forgotten to lose before, he lit a fire all around the cockatrice. The wood blazed, and presently something in the basin caught fire. Edmund saw that it was a sort of liquid that burned. And now the cockatrice stirred it with his tail and flapped his wings in it. Some of it splashed out on Edmund's hand and burned it rather badly. But the cockatrice grew red and strong and happy, and its comb grew scarlet, and its feathers glossy, and it lifted itself up and crowed, "Cock-a-trice-a-doodle-doo!" very loudly and clearly.

Edmund's kindly nature was charmed to see the cockatrice so much improved in health, and he said, "Don't mention it," when the cockatrice began to thank him.

"But what can I do for you?" the creature asked.

"Tell me stories," said Edmund.

"What about?" said the cockatrice.

The Caves and the Cockatrice

"About true things that they don't know at school," said Edmund. So the cockatrice began. He told Edmund about mines and treasures and geological formations, and about gnomes and fairies and dragons, and about glaciers and the Stone Age and the beginning of the world, and about the unicorn and the phoenix, and about magic, black and white.

Edmund ate his eggs and his apple turnover, and listened. When he got hungry again, he said goodbye and went home. But he came again the next day for more stories, and the next day, and the next, for a long time.

He told the boys at school about the cockatrice and his wonderful true tales, and the boys liked the stories. But when he told the master, he was caned for untruthfulness.

"But it's true," said Edmund. "Just you look where the fire burned my hand."

"I see you've been playing with fire – into mischief as usual," said the master, and he caned Edmund harder than ever. The master was ignorant and unbelieving, but I am told that some schoolmasters are not like that.

The Snake-Woman

Flora Annie Steel

Once upon a time, King Ali Mardan went out hunting. As he hunted in the forest above the beautiful Dal lake, which stretches clear and placid between the mountains and the royal town of Srinagar, he came suddenly upon a maiden. She was as lovely as a flower. But she was seated beneath a tree, weeping bitterly. The King went up to the girl and asked her who she was, and how she came to be alone in the wild forest.

"Oh great King," she answered, "I am the Emperor of China's servant girl, and as I wandered about in the grounds of his palace, I lost my way. I do not know how far I have come since, but now I must surely die, for I am weary and hungry."

"You shall not die while I can protect you," said the King, gazing at the beautiful girl. So he told his servants to take her to his summer palace in the Shalimar gardens, where the fountains scatter dewdrops over the beds of flowers, and fruit trees bend over the marble terraces. And there the King speedily became so in love with her that he forgot everything else in the world.

Some weeks later, a wise man visited the palace. Now, the wise man was very clever, and when he saw the King he knew at once all was not right, so he said, "Oh King, you have been good to me and I would like to do you a kind action. So tell me truly – have you always had that white scared face and those stony eyes?"

The King hung his head.

"Tell me truly," said the wise man, "have you a strange woman in your palace?"

Then Ali Mardan, feeling a strange relief in speaking, told the wise man about the finding of the maiden, so lovely and forlorn, in the forest.

"She is no servant girl of the Emperor of China – she is no woman!" said the wise man fearlessly. "She is nothing but a Lamia – the dreadful two hundred-year-old snake monster, which has the power of taking a woman's shape!"

Hearing this, King Ali Mardan was at first angry, for he was madly in love with the stranger. But when the wise man insisted, he at last promised to obey the wise man's orders, and so discover the truth of his words.

Therefore, that same evening, the King ordered two kinds of rice to be made ready for supper and placed in one dish. So one half was sweet rice and the other half was salty rice.

When the King sat down to eat out of the same dish with the Snake-Woman, he turned the salt side towards her and the sweet side towards himself.

She found her portion very salty, but, seeing the King eat his with relish and without remark, finished hers in silence. But after the meal, the Snake-Woman became so dreadfully thirsty that she longed for a drink of water. As there was none in the room, she was forced to go outside.

Now, if a Snake-Woman goes out at

night, she must resume her own monster
form. So King Ali Mardan saw the beautiful
girl change to a deadly, slimy snake that
slid out of the door into the garden. He
followed the snake softly, watching it drink
from every fountain by the way, until it
reached the Dal lake, where it
drank and bathed for hours.

The Snake-Woman

Weird and Wonderful Beasts

King Ali Mardan admitted he believed the truth of the wise man's story, and begged him for help in getting rid of the horror. This the wise man promised to do, if the King would faithfully obey orders.

So they made an oven of a hundred different kinds of metal melted together, and closed by a strong lid and a heavy padlock. This they placed in a shady corner of the garden, fastening it securely to the ground by strong chains. When all was ready, the King said to the Snake-Woman, "My heart's beloved! Let us wander in the gardens alone today and amuse ourselves by cooking our own food."

The King heated the oven very hot and kneaded the bread, but being clumsy at it, he told the Snake-Woman he could do no more, and that she must bake the bread. This she at first refused to do, saying that she disliked ovens. But in the end she gave in and set to work.

Then, just as she stooped over the oven's mouth to turn the loaves, the King, seizing his opportunity, pushed her in and, clapping down the cover, locked and double-locked it.

The King and the wise man piled fuel onto the fire and the oven grew hotter and hotter. So it went on from four o'clock one afternoon to four o'clock the next.

They waited until the oven grew cold and then opened it. Not a trace of the Snake-Woman was to be seen, only a tiny heap of ashes, out of which the wise man took a small, round stone. He gave it to the King, saying, "Whatever you touch with it will turn to gold."

But King Ali Mardan said such a treasure was more than any man's life was worth, since it would bring envy and battle and murder to anyone who owned it. So the King threw the magical snake-stone into the lake, so as not to bring trouble into the world.

TOOTH AND CLAW

Grendel's Mother

Hamilton W Mabie

*The great warrior Beowulf has slain the monster,
Grendel, whose dying body sank beneath the waters of
a dark lake after attacking the lands of the Danish King
Hrothgar. But that is not the end of Beowulf's problems.*

The monster Grendel was dead, but
Grendel's mother still lived. Furious
at the death of her son, she crept to the
great hall and made her way in. She
clutched an earl, the King's dearest friend,

and crushed him in his sleep. The knights leapt up, swords in hand, and the monster hurried to escape.

The aged King felt bitter sorrow when he heard that his dearest friend was killed, and sent for Beowulf. "We have fresh grief this morning," said the King. "My dearest friend and noblest knight is slain. You destroyed Grendel, but another monster has come. I have heard the country folk say that there were two huge fiends to be seen stalking over the moors – one like a woman, the other had the form of a man, but much bigger. It was he they called Grendel. These two haunt a fearful spot, a land of bogs and windy cliffs. A waterfall plunges into the blackness below and twisted trees overhang it. None can tell the depth of the stream.

Even a stag, hunted to death, will face his foes on the bank rather than plunge into those waters. It is a fearful spot. You are our only hope, Beowulf. Dare you enter this horrible haunt?"

Beowulf answered quickly, "Let us track the monster. Each of us must expect death, but he who has the chance should do mighty deeds before it comes. I promise you, Grendel's Mother shall not escape me."

The King sprang up gladly, and Beowulf and his friends set out. Suddenly they saw a clump of gloomy trees, overhanging a dreary pool. A shudder ran through them, for the pool was blood-red.

They sat down by the edge of the pool, while the horn sounded a cheerful blast. In the water were monstrous sea-snakes, and

on jutting points of land were dragons and
strange beasts. They tumbled away, full of
rage at the sound of the horn.

Beowulf was getting ready for the fight.
He covered his body with armour. On his
head he put a white helmet, decorated with

figures of boars worked in silver. His sword was a wonderful treasure with an edge of iron. It had never failed anyone who had needed it in battle.

"Be like a father to my men if I perish," said Beowulf to Hrothgar. "Either I will win fame or death shall take me."

He dashed away, plunging into the pool. It took nearly the whole day before he reached the bottom and, while he was still on his way, the water monster met him. She made a grab at Beowulf and caught him in her talons, but his coat of mail saved him from her fingers. Still Grendel's Mother clutched him tight, and carried him in her arms to the bottom of the lake. Beowulf saw that he was in a great hall, where there was no water, but a strange, unearthly glow.

Grendel's Mother

The fight began straight away, but the sword would not bite – it failed its master in his need. Beowulf threw it away in anger, trusting the strength of his hands. He seized the monster by the shoulders so that she sank down. She recovered quickly and closed in on him. Beowulf staggered and fell, worn out. He stood up again and then truly God helped him. For he saw among the armour on the wall an old sword of huge size, the handiwork of giants. He seized it and struck with all his might, so that Grendel's Mother gave up her life.

His heart was full of gladness and light filled the hall. Beowulf left the body of the monster and saw her son, Grendel, lying there dead. Beowulf cut off his head as a trophy for King Hrothgar, whose men the fiend had killed and eaten.

Now those men who were seated on the banks of the pool, watching with Hrothgar, saw that the water was tinged with blood. Then the old men spoke together of brave Beowulf, saying they feared they would never see him again. The day was passing fast, so they and the King went homewards. Beowulf's men longed, but did not expect, to see their lord and master.

Under the depths, Beowulf was making his way to them. The magic sword melted in his hand until only the handle remained. He brought nothing more with him than the handle and Grendel's head.

Beowulf came to land, bravely swimming. His men thanked God and ran to free him of his armour. Then they marched gladly through the highways to the town. It took four of them to carry Grendel's head. On they went, all fourteen, their captain glorious in their midst. They entered the great hall, startling the King and Queen with the fearful sight of Grendel's head.

Beowulf handed the magic handle to King Hrothgar, who saw that it was the work of giants of old. He spoke to Beowulf, praising him for his courage, and said that he would love him as his son. "Many, many treasures," he said, "must pass from me to you tomorrow. But now, rest and feast."

Gladly Beowulf sat down to the banquet and he liked the thought of the rest.

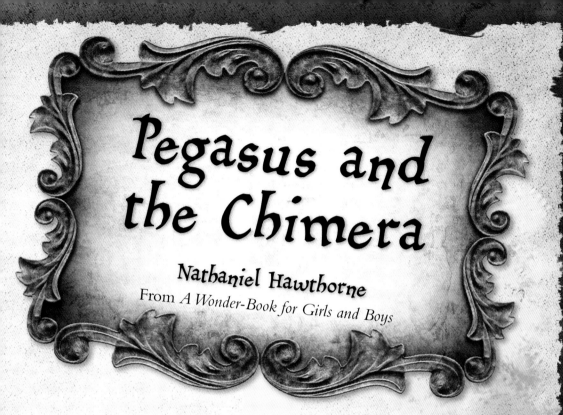

Pegasus and the Chimera

Nathaniel Hawthorne

From *A Wonder-Book for Girls and Boys*

The Greek hero, Bellerophon, has tamed the magical, winged horse Pegasus. Together they have flown to try and defeat the terrible monster, the Chimera.

The winged horse gradually descended with his rider. It was a wild, savage and rocky land with high hills. In the more level part of the country, there were the ruins of houses that had been burned.

'The Chimera must have done this

mischief,' thought Bellerophon. 'But where can the monster be?'

There was nothing unusual to be seen in any of the valleys. Nothing at all, except three spires of black smoke, which came from what appeared to be the mouth of a cavern. The cavern was almost directly beneath the winged horse and his rider.

There seemed to be a heap of strange and terrible creatures curled up within the cavern. The three spires of smoke came from the nostrils of these three heads! Their bodies lay so close together that Bellerophon could not tell them apart. But judging by their heads, one of these creatures was a huge snake, the second a fierce lion and the third an ugly goat.

The lion and the goat were asleep, but

the snake was wide awake and kept staring around him with a great pair of fiery eyes. All at once, Bellerophon started as from a dream and knew it to be the Chimera. The snake, the lion and the goat were not three separate creatures, but one monster!

Here was the terrible three-headed Chimera! Pegasus seemed to know it too and let out a neigh that sounded like the call of a trumpet to battle. At this sound, the three heads reared up and belched out great flashes of flame. The monster flung itself out of the cavern and sprang straight towards Bellerophon, with its immense claws outstretched and its snaky tail twisting itself behind.

If Pegasus had not been as nimble as a bird, both he and his rider would have been overthrown by the Chimera's rush, and the battle ended then and there. But the winged horse was not to be caught. In the twinkling of an eye, he was halfway to the clouds.

The Chimera raised itself up to stand on the tip of its tail, with its talons pawing fiercely in the air and its three heads spluttering fire at Pegasus and his rider. How it roared and hissed and bellowed! Meanwhile, Bellerophon was fitting his shield on his arm and drawing his sword.

"Now, my beloved Pegasus," he whispered in the winged horse's ear, "you must help me to slay this monster. For either the Chimera dies or its three mouths shall have this head of mine!"

Pegasus whinnied and rubbed his nose against his rider's cheek. Then Bellerophon

421

shook the bridle and Pegasus darted down as swift as an arrow, right towards the Chimera's head. As he came within arm's length, Bellerophon made a cut at the monster. Then Pegasus wheeled round to about the same distance from the Chimera as before. Bellerophon now saw that he had cut the goat's head of the monster almost off, so that it dangled down and seemed quite dead.

But the snake's head and the lion's head spat flame, and hissed and roared with a great deal more fury than before.

"Never mind, my brave Pegasus!" cried Bellerophon. "With another stroke like that we will stop its hissing or its roaring."

And again he shook the bridle. The winged horse made another flight towards

Pegasus and the Chimera

the Chimera, and Bellerophon aimed
another stroke at one of the two remaining
heads as he shot by. But, this time, neither
he nor Pegasus escaped so well as at first.
With one of its claws, the Chimera gave
Bellerophon a deep scratch in his shoulder.
On his side, Bellerophon had wounded the

lion's head of the monster, so that it now hung down and sent out gasps of thick black smoke. The snake's head, which was the only one now left, was twice as fierce as before. It belched forth shoots of fire five hundred yards long.

Then Bellerophon shook the bridle, shouted loudly and guided Pegasus straight at the monster's hideous front. It seemed just a dazzle and a flash before Bellerophon was at close grips with the enemy.

The Chimera, after losing its second head, was red–hot with pain and rage. It opened its jaws to such a width that Pegasus might almost have flown right down its throat. It then shot out a tremendous blast of its fiery breath, and surrounding Bellerophon and his horse in

flame and singeing the wings of Pegasus,
scorching off one side of the young man's
golden hair, and making them both far
hotter than was comfortable. But this was
nothing to what followed.

The Chimera gave a spring and flung its
huge body right upon poor Pegasus. It
clung round him and tied up its snaky tail
in a knot. Up flew Pegasus, higher, higher,
higher, above the mountain peaks, above
the clouds, and almost out of sight of the
solid earth. But still the monster kept its
hold. Meanwhile, Bellerophon, turning
about, found himself face to face with the
Chimera, and could only avoid being
scorched to death by holding up his shield.
Over the upper edge of the shield, he looked
into the savage eyes of the monster.

But the Chimera was so mad and wild
with pain, that it did not guard itself well.
Perhaps the best way to fight a Chimera is
by getting as close to it as you can! In its

efforts to stick its horrible iron claws into its enemy, the creature left itself quite exposed. Seeing this, Bellerophon thrust his sword up to its handle into the Chimera's cruel heart.

Immediately the snaky tail untied its knot. The monster let go its hold of Pegasus and fell from that great height downwards, while its fire burned fiercer than ever. The Chimera fell out of the sky aflame and, because it was nightfall before it reached the earth, was mistaken for a shooting star or a comet. Nothing else was ever seen of the dreadful Chimera.

When Bellerophon had won the victory, he bent forwards and kissed Pegasus, tears in his eyes. Then he slipped off the enchanted bridle from the head of the marvellous steed.

"Be free for ever more, my Pegasus!" Bellerophon cried, with a shade of sadness in the tone of his voice. But Pegasus rested his head on Bellerophon's shoulder and would not take flight.

The Buggane of Glen Meay Waterfall

Sophia Morrison

*A buggane is said to be a huge, hairy monster
from the Isle of Man, with great claws and tusks.*

There was once a wife of a decent,
quiet, hardworking man. There was
no one but herself and her husband. They
had a nice little cottage on which they
grazed a cow and a few sheep, and grew
enough potatoes to last them the winter.
The man went fishing when things were

429

slack on land. But for all that they were not comfortable, for work as hard as the man might at his farming and fishing, he was kept poor by his lazy wife.

The woman was fond of lying in bed in the morning. The neighbours said that she wore out more blankets than shoes! Many a day her husband would go out early, as hungry as a hawk, without any food inside him. One morning, when he came in from work, his wife was still not up. And when he came in for dinner, she was still not up, so the man said to her, "Wife, the Buggane will get you sure enough, if you don't mend your ways!"

"What's a buggane?" she asked.

"Ah," he said. "It's a big, black, hairy monster that lies under the waterfall."

The Buggane of Glen Meay Waterfall

"Aw, hold your tongue, man. You don't frighten me with your bugganes," shouted the woman.

In the evening, the man left the house to go out fishing. As soon as he had gone, the woman thought that she should bake some bread, as she had only the end of the loaf left for breakfast.

Now, none of the magical folk can stand lazy ways, and baking after sunset is the one thing they won't accept. She who does so will meet their revenge.

The woman set to work to bake barley bread and flour cake. She got some flour out of the barrel, put it on the round table, and put salt and water on it. Then she kneaded the meal and clapped a loaf out as thin as a coin with her hands. But she was only an average baker, one of the sort that has to use a knife to make the cake the right shape. Just at that moment, she heard the sound of something heavy lumbering up to the door.

After a few seconds, something fumbled at the handle of the door. Then something knocked high up on the door and a voice, like the thick, gruff voice of a giant, was heard saying, "Open, open for me." The woman made no answer. Again there was a loud knock on the door and a big, hoarse voice cried, "Woman of the house, open for me."

Then the door burst open and what should she see but a great, big, ugly beast of a buggane, rushing in mad with rage. Without as much as a, "By your leave," he

The Buggane of Glen Meay Waterfall

made one grab at her, clutched hold of her by her apron, and swung her on his shoulder and away with him.

Before she knew where she was, the beast

rushed her across the fields and down the hill, till he brought her to the top of the big waterfall of Glen Meay.

As the Buggane tore down the hill, the woman felt the ground tremble under his feet and the noise of the waterfall filled her ears. And, there in front of her, she saw the stream turn to white spray as it came leaping down the rocks.

The Buggane swung her in the air to throw her into the deep pool, and she thought that her last hour had come. Then, all at once, she remembered the knife that she held in her hand! Quick as thought, she cut the string of her apron and down she tumbled to the ground, rolling over and over down the hill.

The Buggane, with all the speed he had

The Buggane of Glen Meay Waterfall

in him, dived forwards head first down the rushing waterfall. He went head over heels and down to the bottom of the pool with a splash you'd have heard half a mile away. She heard him give a roar, "Rumbyl, rumbyl, sambyl, I thought I had the lazy dirt, and I have but the edge of her skirt!"

That was the last that was ever seen of the Buggane.

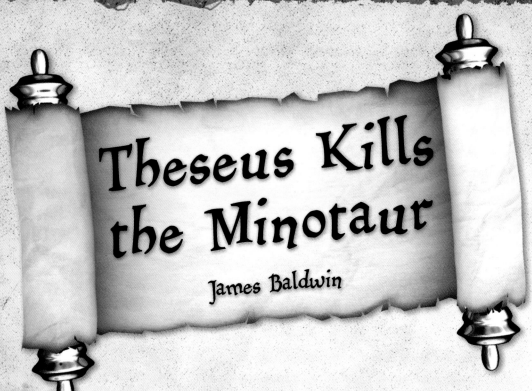

Theseus Kills the Minotaur

James Baldwin

The kingdom of Athens has been defeated by King Minos of Crete. He has demanded that every year they must send seven girls and seven boys to Crete, to be eaten by the Minotaur, who lives in a labyrinth.

In every house in Athens there was sorrow and dread. The springtime had come again. The black-sailed ship was ready for another voyage. But the young prince, Theseus, cried, "I myself will go with these young men and maidens, and I will slay the monster, Minotaur."

"No!" said the King, "For no one who is thrust into the den of the Minotaur ever comes out again."

"Don't you call me the hope of Athens?" said Theseus. "Then how can I do otherwise than go?" And he began at once to make himself ready.

Then the people, and King Egeus himself, went down to the shore to say goodbye to the young men and maidens who had been chosen to go. Everyone except Theseus wept and was broken-hearted.

"I will come again, father," Theseus said.

"I will hope that you may," said the old King. "If when this ship returns, I see a white sail spread above the black one, then I

shall know that you are alive and well.
But if I see only the black one, it will
tell me that you have perished."

And now the vessel was loosened from
its moorings and the north wind filled the
sail. The seven young men and seven
maidens were carried over the sea, towards
the dreadful death that awaited them in far
distant Crete.

At last, the black ship reached the end of
its voyage. The young people were set
ashore, and a party of soldiers led them
through the streets towards the prison,
where they were to stay until the day after.
They passed close by the palace gate, and
in it stood King Minos himself and his
daughter Ariadne, the fairest of the women
of Crete.

Theseus Kills the Minotaur

"Indeed, those are noble young fellows," said the King.

"Yes, too noble to feed the vile Minotaur," said Ariadne. Ariadne said no more. Yet she thought that she had never seen anyone who looked so much like a hero as young Theseus. How tall he was, and how handsome! All through that night Ariadne lay awake and thought of the hero, and then she began to lay plans for setting him free.

439

Tooth and Claw

At the earliest peep of day, while everybody else was asleep, Ariadne ran out of the palace and hurried to the prison. As she was the King's daughter, the jailer opened the door and allowed her to go in. She took Theseus aside and told him of a plan which she had made to save him. Then she gave him a sharp sword and hid it underneath his cloak, telling him that with it alone he could hope to kill the Minotaur.

"And here is a ball of silken thread," Ariadne said. "As soon as you go into the Labyrinth where the monster is kept, fasten one end of the thread to the stone doorpost, and then unwind it as you go along. When you have killed the Minotaur, you have only to follow the thread and it will lead you back to the door. Meanwhile, I will see that your ship is ready to sail."

Theseus thanked the beautiful princess. He promised her that if he should live to go back to Athens, she would go with him and be his wife. Then Ariadne hastened away.

As soon as the sun was up, the guards came to lead the young prisoners to the Labyrinth. They did not see the sword that Theseus had under his cloak, nor the ball of silk that he held in his closed hand.

The guards led the young men and maidens into the Labyrinth, turning here and there, back and forth, a thousand different times, until it seemed certain that they could never find their way out again. Then the guards, by a secret passage which they alone knew, went out and left them, as they had left many others before.

TOOTH AND CLAW

For hours they stood there, hearing no sound and seeing nothing but the smooth, high walls on either side of the passage.

At last, they heard a bellowing, low and faint as though far away. They listened and soon heard it again, a little louder and very fierce and dreadful.

"He is coming!" cried Theseus, and he ran forwards to meet the beast. Soon the Minotaur came into view, rushing down the passage towards Theseus and roaring terribly. He was twice as tall as a man. His head was like that of a bull, with huge, sharp horns, fiery eyes and a mouth as large as a lion's. When the Minotaur saw Theseus he put his head down and rushed forwards, bellowing.

Theseus ran up to the Minotaur and

443

thrust the sword into its heart. Theseus was away again before the beast could harm him. A great stream of blood gushed from the wound, and very soon the Minotaur was dead.

Then the young men and maidens ran to Theseus and kissed his hands and feet, thanking him for his great deed. As it was already growing dark, Theseus told them to follow him while he wound up the silken thread that was to lead them out of the Labyrinth.

They went through a thousand rooms and courts and winding ways. At midnight, they came to the outer door and saw the city lying in the moonlight before them. Only a little way off was the seashore, where the black ship that had brought them to Crete was moored. The door was wide open and beside it stood Ariadne, waiting for them.

"The wind is fair, the sea is smooth and the sailors are ready," she whispered. Ariadne took the arm of Theseus, and they all went together through the silent streets to the ship.

When the morning dawned, they were far out to sea and, looking back from the deck of the little vessel, only the white tops of the Cretan mountains could be seen.

When King Minos arose from his sleep, he did not know that the young men and maidens had got safely out of the Labyrinth. But when Ariadne could not be found, he thought that robbers had carried her away. He sent soldiers out to search for

her among the hills and mountains, never
dreaming that she was now well on the way
towards distant Athens.

Many days passed, and at last the
searchers returned and said that the princess
could be found nowhere. The King covered
his head and wept, and said, "Now, indeed,
I have lost my greatest treasure!"

Meanwhile, King Egeus of Athens had sat
day after day on a rock by the shore,
looking and watching for a ship coming
from the south. At last the vessel with
Theseus and his companions came into
sight, but it still carried only the black sail.
In their joy, the young men had forgotten
to raise the white one.

"Alas! Alas! My son has perished!"
moaned Egeus. He fainted, fell forwards

into the sea and was drowned. That sea, from then until now, has been called by his name, the Aegean Sea.

And so Theseus became King of Athens.

The Buggane of the Church

Sophia Morrison

A long time ago, some monks came to the broad, rough meadow that is between dark Greeba Mountain and the high road. They chose a nice place and set up a church on it. But they did not know about the power of the Buggane, who had his haunt in the mountain. The Buggane was very angry and he said to himself, "I'll have no peace night or day with their

The Buggane of the Church

jingling bells if I let them finish the building." And, as he had nothing else to do, he thought he would amuse himself by tossing off the roof of the church.

So, when the roof of the church was first put on, a dreadful sound was heard that very night. When the people of Greeba got up early next morning, they found their church roofless, and planks and broken beams all around the place.

After a time and with great effort, the roof was put on again. But when it was on, a great storm arose in the night and it was blown down from the walls, exactly as had happened before. This fall put fear in the people, for they were sure now that it was the evil Buggane himself that was doing the mischief. But, though they were terrified, they decided to make one more attempt, and the third roof was nearly finished.

Now, there was a brave little tailor living about a mile from Greeba. Because he did not have much money, he made a bet with a friend that when the new roof was on, he would not only spend the first night in the church, he would also make a pair of breeches there. The bet was taken up eagerly, as it was hoped that if the roof was up for one night, it would be left on.

So Tim – that was the name of the tailor – went to the church on the very first evening after the new roof had been put on. He started just when the shadow was beginning to get grey by the hedges. Tim took with him cloth, needle and thread, thimble and scissors. He entered the church boldly, lit a couple of big candles, and looked all over the building to see that everything was right. Then he locked the door so that there was no way to get in. He cut out the cloth and, seating himself cross-legged, he set to work at the breeches.

With a long thread and needle, Tim bent low over his work, his fingers moving backwards and forwards. The breeches had got to be finished or he would lose his bet, so he stitched away as fast as he could, thinking about the money the people would have to give him.

The tailor's courage rose high and he said to himself, "It's all foolishness about the Buggane."

But at that very minute the ground heaved under him and rumbling sounds came up from below. The sounds grew louder underneath and Tim glanced quickly up. All of a sudden, a great big head broke a hole through the stone floor just before the tailor, and came rising up slowly through the hole.

The head was covered with a mane of coarse, black hair. It had eyes like torches and glittering sharp tusks. When the head had risen above the stone floor, the fiery eyes glared fiercely at Tim. The big, ugly, red mouth opened wide, and a dreadful voice said, "You rascal, what business have you here?"

Tim paid no attention, but worked harder still at the breeches, for he knew he had no time to lose.

"Do you see this big head of mine?"

The Buggane of the Church

yelled the Buggane loudly.

"I see, I see!" replied Tim, mockingly.

Up came a big, broad pair of shoulders, then a thick arm shot out and a great fist shook in the tailor's face.

Tooth and Claw

"Do you see my long arms?" roared the terrible voice.

"I see, I see!" answered Tim, boldly.

The Buggane kept rising and rising up through the hole, until the horrible, ugly, hairy form, covered with wrinkles, had risen quite out of the ground.

"Do you see this big body of mine?" roared the Buggane, angry that Tim showed no fear of him.

"I see, I see!" replied the tailor, while at the same time stitching with all his might at the breeches.

"Do you see my sharp claws?" roared the Buggane in a more angry voice than before.

"I see, I see!" answered the tailor again, without raising his eyes and continuing to pull the thread with all his might.

The Buggane of the Church

"Do you see my large foot?" thundered
the Buggane, drawing up one big foot and
putting it down on the stone floor with a
thud that made the walls shake.

"I see, I see!" replied the tailor as before, stitching hard at the breeches and taking long stitches.

Lifting up his other foot, the Buggane, in a furious rage, yelled, "Do you see my rough arms, my bony fingers, my hard fists, my—?"

Before the Buggane could utter another word or pull his other foot out of the ground, the tailor quickly jumped up and made two stitches together. The breeches were at last finished, so then with one large spring the tailor made a leap through the nearest window.

But scarcely was he outside the walls of the church, when down fell the new roof with a terrible crash, which made the tailor run a great deal more nimbly than he had ever run before.

Hearing the Buggane's fiendish guffaws of laughter behind him, he took to his heels and sped along Douglas Road, the breeches under his arms and the furious Buggane in full chase.

The tailor made for Marown Church, which was only a little distance away, and knew he would be safe if he could only reach the churchyard.

Tim ran faster still, reached the wall, leapt over it like a hunted hare, and fell weary and spent upon the grass. The tailor was under the shadow of the church, where the Buggane did not have the power to follow him.

So furious was the monster at this that he seized his own head with his two hands,

TOOTH AND CLAW

The Buggane of the Church

tore it off his body and sent it flying over the wall after the tailor. The head burst at the tailor's feet with a terrific explosion. With that, the Buggane vanished and was never seen or heard of again. The tailor was not hurt and he won the bet, for no one grumbled at the few long stitches put into the breeches.

And as for the church, its roof was never replaced. It stands in the green meadow under the shadow of rocky Greeba Mountain, and there its grey, roofless ruins are to be found now.

Zelinda and the Monster

Thomas Frederick Crane

*This is an Italian version of the
well-loved story 'Beauty and the Beast'.*

There was once a poor man who had
three daughters. It happened that he
had to go on a journey, and before
departing he asked his three daughters if
they would like some small presents. Rosina
asked her father for a dress, Marietta asked
him for a shawl, but Zelinda was satisfied

460

with a handsome rose.

The poor man set out on his journey early the next day. When he arrived at the fair, he quickly bought what he needed. Afterwards, he easily found Rosina's dress and Marietta's shawl, but at that season he could not find a rose for his Zelinda.

However, he took the first road he came to and, after journeying for a while, arrived at a handsome garden enclosed by high walls. As the gate was partly open, he entered quietly. He found the garden filled with every kind of flower and plant, and in a corner was a tall rose bush, full of beautiful rosebuds.

Wherever he looked, no living soul appeared from whom he might ask for a rose as a gift or for money. So the poor

man, without thinking, stretched out his
hand and picked a rose for his Zelinda.
Scarcely had he pulled the flower from
the stalk when there arose a great noise and
flames darted from the earth. All at once
there appeared a terrible monster, who
hissed with all his
might, "What have
you done? You
must die, because
you have

destroyed my rose bush."

The poor man, more than half dead with terror, began to weep and beg for mercy on his knees, saying, "Let me depart. I have a family, and if I am killed, they will suffer."

But the monster, more wicked than ever, responded, "Listen, someone must die. Either bring me the girl that asked for the rose, or I will kill you this very moment." He did not let the poor man go until he had sworn to bring his daughter Zelinda to him in the garden.

Imagine how downhearted that poor man returned home! He gave his oldest daughters their presents, and Zelinda her rose. But his face was as white as though he had arisen from the dead. The girls, in terror, asked him what had happened and whether he had met with any misfortune. At last the poor man, weeping bitterly, told them of the misfortunes of that unhappy journey, and on what condition he had been able finally to return home. "In short," he exclaimed, "either Zelinda or I must be eaten by the monster."

Zelinda simply said, "I will go to the monster. Yes, Papa, take me to the garden, and the Lord's will be done."

The next day, Zelinda and her sorrowful father began their journey and at night-time they arrived at the garden gate. When they entered they saw, as usual, no one, but they beheld a lordly palace all lit up and the doors wide open.

When the two travellers entered the hall, four marble statues with lit torches in their hands came down from their pedestals. They accompanied them up the stairs to a large hall, where a table was lavishly spread. The travellers, who were very hungry, sat down and began to eat. When they had finished, Zelinda and her father were so weary that they slept all night.

At daybreak Zelinda and her father arose and descended to the garden. They began to look for the monster. When they came to the rose bush, he appeared in all his frightful ugliness. Zelinda, on seeing him, became pale with fear and her limbs trembled. But the monster looked at her with his great, fiery eyes, and afterwards said to the poor man, "Very well. You have kept your word and I am satisfied. Now depart and leave me alone here with the young girl."

At this command, the old man thought
he should die, and Zelinda stood there
with her eyes full of tears. But no matter
what the man said, the monster insisted, and
in the end the poor man left, leaving his
dear Zelinda in the monster's power.

When the monster was alone with
Zelinda he managed to appear quite
friendly. He saw that she had everything
she needed, and every day, talking with her
in the garden, he asked her, "Do you love
me, Zelinda? Will you be my wife?"

The young girl always answered him in
the same way, "I like you, sir, but I will
never be your wife."

One day, the monster called Zelinda in
haste and said, "Listen, Zelinda, if you do
not agree to marry me it is fated that your

father must die. He is ill and near the end of his life, and you will not be able to see him again. See whether I am telling you the

truth." And, drawing out an enchanted mirror, the monster showed Zelinda her father on his deathbed.

At that spectacle, Zelinda, in despair and half mad with grief, cried, "Oh, save my father, for mercy's sake! Let me kiss him once more before he dies. Yes, yes, I promise you I will be your faithful and constant wife without delay. But save my father from death."

Hardly had Zelinda uttered these words when suddenly, right before her eyes, the monster was transformed into a very handsome young man. Zelinda was shocked and amazed by this sudden, unexpected change.

The young man took Zelinda by the hand and said, "Know, dear Zelinda, that I am the son of the King of the Oranges. An old witch touched me and changed me into the terrible monster I was. She

condemned me to be hidden in this rose
bush until a beautiful girl consented to
become my wife."

The Norka

Andrew Lang

Once upon a time, there lived a king and queen who had three sons. Now, the King had a park where he kept wild animals of different kinds. Into that park, there used to come a huge beast with mighty claws and red teeth. Its name was Norka, and it would do fearful mischief, killing and eating some of the animals every night.

The Norka

The King did all he could, but he was unable to destroy the beast. So at last he called his sons together and said, "I will give half of my kingdom to whoever destroys the Norka."

Well, the eldest son undertook the task. As soon as it was night, he took his weapons and set out. But before he reached the park, he went into a tavern, and there he spent the whole night. When he came to his senses it was too late – the day had already dawned. The next day, the second son went and did just the same, and their father scolded them both.

On the third day, the youngest son undertook the task. His brothers laughed at him, feeling sure he wouldn't do anything. But he went straight into the park, and sat

TOOTH AND CLAW

down on the grass in such a position that the moment he fell asleep, his weapons would prick him and he would wake up.

Presently, the midnight hour sounded. The earth began to shake and the Norka came rushing up. It burst right through the fence into the park, so huge was it. The Prince pulled himself together, leapt to his feet and went straight at the beast. It fled away and the Prince ran after it. Then the beast stopped at a great white stone, tilted it up and escaped down a long hole to the other world.

The Prince went home and told his father all that had happened. He asked him to have a leather rope plaited, long enough to reach to the other world. His father ordered this to be done.

When the rope was made, the Prince and his brothers went back to the place where the Norka had disappeared under the stone. The Prince said, "Now, brothers, who is going to lift this stone?"

Neither of them could so much as stir it, but as soon as the Prince touched it, away it flew, though it was ever so big – as big as a hill. When he had flung the stone aside, he spoke a second time to his brothers, saying, "Well, brothers, farewell! Lower me into the other world and don't go away from here. As soon as the cord is jerked, pull it up."

His brothers lowered him accordingly, and when he had reached the other world, underneath the earth, he went on his way.

The Prince walked and walked until he saw, standing before him, a palace made of copper. He entered the courtyard and went indoors. In one of the rooms a dinner was laid out. He sat down and dined.

Presently, there came in a lady, more beautiful than can be imagined anywhere but in a fairy tale. When she saw the Prince she was delighted with him, and said, "Why, O Prince – you shall be my husband. Why have you come here?"

Then the Prince told her all that had happened, and she said, "The beast that you wish to overcome is my brother. He is staying with my second sister, who lives not far from here in a silver palace. I bound up the wounds that you gave him."

After this they drank and enjoyed themselves. They talked for a long time and then the Prince said goodbye. He went on to the second sister who lived in the silver palace, and with her he also stayed awhile. The second sister told him that her brother Norka was at her youngest sister's house.

So the Prince went on to the youngest

sister, who lived in a golden palace. She told him that her brother was at that time asleep on the blue sea. She gave the Prince a sword of steel and a drink of the Water of Strength, and she told him to go and cut off Norka's head with a single stroke. With this, the Prince went on his way.

When the Prince came to the blue sea, he saw the Norka asleep on a stone in the middle of the sea. When it snored, the water was rough for

The Norka

seven miles around. The Prince went up to it and struck it on the head with his sword. After killing the beast, the Prince went back again, picking up all three sisters on the way, to take into the upper world. For they all loved him and would not be separated from him. His brothers pulled him up, and the three brothers and the three sisters went home. Afterwards, three weddings were celebrated, and the youngest prince married the princess of the copper castle.

The Great Spider

William Elliot Griffis

Once upon a time in Japan, the brave warrior Raiko fell sick, and daily grew weaker and paler. When his enemy demons found this out, they sent the three-eyed, shape-changing imp, called Mitsumé Kozo, to plague him.

This imp, which had a snout like a hog's, three monstrous blue eyes and a mouth full of tusks, was glad that the brave soldier

could no longer fight. He would approach
the sick man in his chamber, leer horribly at
him, loll out his tongue, and pull down the
lids of his eyes with his hairy fingers until
the sight sickened
Raiko more
and more.

But Raiko, well or ill, always slept with
his trusty sword under his pillow. By
pretending to be afraid and cowering under
the bedclothes, he let the imp grow bolder
and bolder. When the imp was near the bed,

Raiko drew his blade and cut him across his huge nose. This made the imp howl, and he ran away, leaving tracks of blood.

When Raiko's friend, Tsuna, and his band heard of their brave master's exploit, they came to congratulate him, and offered to hunt out the monster and destroy him.

They followed the red drops until they came to a cavern in the mountains. Entering this, they saw in the gloom a spider, six feet high, with legs as long as a fishing pole and as thick as a daikon radish. Two great yellow eyes glared at them like lamps. They noticed a great, gaping wound, as if done by a sword, on his snout.

It was a horrible, nasty, hairy thing to fight with swords, since to get near enough, they would be in danger of the creature's

The Great Spider

claws. So Tsuna went and chopped down a tree as thick as a man's leg, leaving the roots on, while his comrades prepared a rope to tie up the monster like a fly in a web. Then with a loud yell, Tsuna rushed at the spider, knocked it down with a blow, and held it down with the tree and roots, so it could not bite or use its claws.

Seeing this, his comrades rushed in and bound the monster's legs tight to its body, so that it could not move. Drawing their swords, they passed them through its body and finished him. Returning in triumph to the city, they found their dear captain recovered from his illness.

Raiko thanked his brave warriors for their exploits, made a feast for them and gave them many presents.

The Twin Children of the Sun

Egerton R Young

An Algonquin American Indian folk tale

Long ago, there were great monsters on this earth. Some of them were enormous animals and fiercer than any that now exist. They lay in wait and caught children and even grown-up people, as wild beasts now catch their prey.

These people were worshippers of the sun, whom they called the great Sun Father. Some tribes still have their sun dances in his honour. When he saw that the people were in such great trouble, he decided to try and help them. So he disguised himself, came down to the earth and married a beautiful woman. They had lovely twin boys, whose names were Sesigizit, the older, and Ooseemeeid, the younger. Their sun father disappeared as soon as they were born, going to the far Eastland.

When the boys were big enough, their mother brought out of hiding a couple of bows, quivers full of arrows and some magic sticks, and gave them to the boys.

"These were left for you by your father," their mother said. "Before he went away, he said that they were to be given to you as soon as you were able to use them."

The children were, of course, very

anxious to try their bows and arrows and magic sticks. So they decided to go off on a hunting expedition.

They were warned by their anxious mother not to go to the east, as there was a narrow lake there, to which many evil creatures came for water, especially a great monster wolf that had eaten many people. Yet the boys immediately started off in that direction, for, like some other boys, they did not always obey even their mother. It was noon before they reached the lake. At first, as they examined it, everything seemed very quiet and still.

"Mother must have been mistaken," Sesigizit said to Ooseemeeid, "for I do not see any living thing here."

But as they wandered farther along the

shore, Ooseemeeid suddenly cried out, "O, see that great wolf on the other side!"

They dropped down as quickly as they could, but the fierce brute had already caught sight of them. He was very much larger than any of the wolves that now howl in the dark forests. The boys shot their arrows at him, but the wolf was only slightly wounded, for he was wearing armour made out of bones. He was very angry about their attacks, and he picked up a magic stick and threw it at them. The two boys threw themselves upon the ground so that it passed over them.

The wolf seized his remaining stick, for he only had two, and he threw it with all his power at the boys. This time they both jumped high up from the ground and the stick passed under them.

It was the two boys' turn now, and they both threw their magic sticks with such force that the great, bony armour of the wolf was crushed in and he was killed.

"Where have you been?" asked their

anxious mother when the two boys
returned home.

"We have been to the lake," they replied.

Then the boys told her of their battle
with the great wolf and how they had killed
him. They also showed her his heart, which
they had brought home with them.

She was very excited and called the
people together. There was great rejoicing
at the death of this terrible wolf.

Some time after, Sesigizit and
Ooseemeeid asked their mother if she knew
where any good, tough wood suitable for
making bows and arrows grew.

Her answer was, "Far away in the
foothills is a canyon, where a forest of just
such wood is growing. But the path that
leads to it is narrow, and a great monster

giant sits guard, who kills and throws into the ravine everyone who goes there. And in addition, there is a fierce mountain lioness prowling around somewhere on the route, and she has already killed many people and carried them off to her den."

The boys set off, but they had not gone very far when they met the great mountain lioness. Ooseemeeid asked her if she knew the way to the canyon where the good wood grew.

"Yes," she replied. "I am going that way and I will show you the route." She said this because she wished to trick the two boys into walking near to her den, and then she would kill them.

So she led them until they came to a place where the path wound on a narrow shelf of rock around the mountainside. Here the monster lioness asked the boys to walk on ahead of her, but they refused, saying that they had been taught never to walk in front of their elders.

When they were in the most dangerous part of the pass, the boys pretended to be very frightened and asked to walk between her and the mountainside. They seemed now to be so scared that the lioness never thought they were planning anything. So she walked on the outer edge of the pass and let them have the inside. She also allowed them to put their hands on her, as though to steady themselves.

When they came to the most dangerous spot, where it was so narrow that even a mountain lion had to be careful, the boys

both gave her a great shove, and sent her
over the side of the narrow rocky ledge.
Down she fell – to be dashed to pieces
thousands of feet below.

The great giant had heard the boys'
shout of triumph when they had destroyed
the mountain lioness, and it made him very

angry, for he hated any noise.

When the monster giant saw the small boys, he was at first inclined to laugh at them. But when they had come near enough to shoot their magic arrows at him, he soon began to roar with the stinging pain they gave him.

The giant began tearing up great rocks and stones, and tried to crush the boys by hurling these at them. Here, the boys' father, the sun, came to their help. He shone so fiercely into the eyes of the great monster giant that he was unable to see, and the boys easily kept out of the way.

The monster giant was so big that the arrows of the boys seemed only like pins and needles sticking into him, and they began to fear that their quivers would be

The Twin Children of the Sun

emptied before they had conquered him.

So they waited until the giant stooped down, struggling to loosen a huge rock from the earth. Then Sesigizit threw his magic stick with all his power. It struck the giant on the top of his head with such force that it broke off a piece of his skull. The next instant, Ooseemeeid fired one of his arrows so accurately that it pierced the giant's brain, through the spot left exposed.

With a roar of rage and pain, the great monster giant fell, rolled down into the deep canyon and died.

After collecting the giant's big flint knife, which hung from his belt, the boys hurried into the canyon and gathered a lot of fine wood for arrow shafts. Then they returned to their mother. When she asked them where they had been, the boys replied that they had been to the canyon, and that they had killed both the mountain lioness and the great giant.

At first she could hardly believe this, but as they had brought the paws of the lioness and the flint knife of the great giant, why, she just had to believe it. How the people rejoiced to be rid of these monsters.

The Giant Centipede

A traditional Japanese tale

One day, a great warrior was striding
out in search of adventures, for he
could not bear to be idle. So he took
his mighty bow and quiver, stuck
his two curved swords into his
sash and took the high road
out of town. He had not
gone far when he
came to a bridge

The Giant Centipede

spanning one end of a beautiful lake. As he stepped onto the bridge, he saw in the twilight a shape blocking his way. He realized it was a huge dragon. Its body was as big as a whale, and its huge claws were as long and as sharp as swords. Its tail lay curled around the bridge. The monster seemed to be asleep, and as it breathed, fire and smoke came out of its nostrils.

At first, the warrior hesitated, feeling fear at the thought of this monster. But he told himself if he turned back now he could never hold his head up again. So he stepped firmly onto the body of the dragon, then climbed over it, ready at any moment to draw his sword if the dragon should start to stir. But it didn't move and the warrior walked on his way.

He had only gone a few steps when he heard someone calling him back. He turned around and was amazed to see that the monster dragon had entirely disappeared, and in its place was an ordinary man, who was bowing to the ground. While the warrior was puzzling over what it meant, the man came up to him and, bowing low, said, "Forgive me. May I speak to you? I wish to beg for help from you."

"If there is anything I can do to help you, I will most certainly do so," answered the warrior, "but first, tell me who you are. Where is the dragon I passed just now? What has happened to it?"

"I am the Dragon King of the Lake, and I live in this lake beneath the bridge. For many days I have waited on the bridge in the shape of a horrible dragon, in the hope that some strong, brave man would come along. You are the first man I have found able to go over me without fear, so I knew at once that you were a man of great courage. I beg you to help me."

"My sword is at your service." said the warrior. "What can I do to help you?"

"I want to beg for your help as the noble

warrior that your actions clearly show you to be. Will you help to kill my deadly enemy, the monster centipede, who lives on the mountain beyond, and who has devoured so many of my people, to our great sorrow?" The Dragon King pointed to a high peak on the opposite shore of the lake. Then he started to tell his story.

"I have lived a long time in my kingdom under the lake, and I have children and grandchildren. For many years, our lives were blessed with great happiness and I ruled my people with a tender care. But now our lives are made a misery by a monster centipede that comes every night and attacks my people. Its cruel claws snatch whoever they can and the centipede carries them off to eat. It has taken our

The Giant Centipede

babies, our honoured grandmothers and the young men who attempt to fight it. Its teeth are as sharp and as big as spearheads, and where its pincers grip, they hold fast. Our warriors have tried in vain to protect the town and many noble men have died. I beg you to kill my enemy the centipede."

The warrior felt very sorry for the Dragon King and promised to do what he could to help him. The warrior asked where the centipede lived, so that he might attack the creature at once. The Dragon King replied that its home was on the mountain peaks, but that every night it came down the path to the lake, nosing around for people to eat. Then the Dragon King invited the warrior to follow him to his home under the lake.

TOOTH AND CLAW

He took the warrior in his arms and
plunged into the lake. As they dropped
down, the waters parted to let them pass,
and the man and the King arrived dry at

The Giant Centipede

the magnificent palace at the bottom of the
lake. The walls were mother of pearl and
the floor was tiled in the silvery blue of
mussel shell.

The warrior was amazed at the feast that
was spread for him. The dishes were
crystallized seaweed and the chopsticks
were of the rarest ebony. The hours flew by
till midnight. The Dragon King was about
to toast the warrior when the palace was
suddenly shaken by a *tramp, tramp, tramp*, as
if a mighty army had begun to march not
far away.

The warrior and his host sprang to their
feet and the Dragon King cried, "Quick! It
is the centipede!"

They clasped arms, and the Dragon King
pushed upwards and swam powerfully to

the surface of the lake. As they broke through the water, they saw two glowing balls of fire approaching the lake.

"The centipede! The centipede!" cried the Dragon King. "Those two balls of fire are its eyes. It is coming for its prey! Now is the time to kill it."

The warrior stared where his host pointed and, in the dim light of the evening, behind the two balls of fire, he saw the long body of an enormous centipede, winding round the mountains.

He took up his bow from behind him and reached into his quiver, where he noticed that he had only three arrows left. 'That should be enough,' he thought. He took the bow and, fitting an arrow to the notch, took careful aim and let fly.

505

Tooth and Claw

The arrow hit the monster centipede right in the middle of its head, but then fell to the ground.

Unworried, the warrior took his second arrow, fitted it to the notch of the bow and let fly. Again the arrow hit the mark, only to then fall to the ground. The centipede could not be killed by arrows! When the Dragon King saw this, he began to tremble with fear.

The warrior saw that he had now only one arrow left in his quiver, and if this one failed he was lost. He looked across the waters. The huge centipede had wound its horrid body seven times round the mountain, as it followed the path down, and would soon be at the lake.

Then suddenly the warrior remembered

that he had heard that human saliva was deadly to centipedes. Could it possibly work on anything this large and horrible? He decided to try his last chance. So, taking his last arrow and first putting the end of it in his mouth, he fitted the notch to his bow, took careful aim once more and let fly.

This time the arrow hit the centipede right in the middle of its head again, but instead of falling away harmlessly as before, it stuck into the creature's brain. Then with a mighty shudder, the snaky body stopped moving. The fiery light of its great eyes and hundred feet darkened to a dull glare, like the sunset of a stormy day, and then went out in blackness.

A great darkness now overspread the heavens. The thunder rolled, the lightning flashed and the wind roared in fury, and it seemed as if the world was coming to an end. Great waves roared over the lake, and the palace was shaken to its foundation.

At last, the dreadful night was over. Day dawned beautiful and clear. The centipede was gone from the mountain.

Then all the inhabitants of the palace came out with joy and the warrior pointed to the lake. There lay the body of the dead centipede, floating on the water, which was dyed red with its blood.

The whole town came and bowed down before the warrior, calling him their preserver and the bravest warrior in all Japan. They heaped him with gifts – swords with handles of finely wrought gold and silver, painted drums, carved jade

The Giant Centipede

ornaments, great brass rice bowls, and a
bow inset with rubies and coral. They
dressed him in silks and the softest, finest
linens, and invited him to stay with them
for as long as he liked. And that night, a
joyous feast was held in the palace under
the lake.

About the Authors

James Baldwin
1841–1925
At the age of 41, James Baldwin published his first book, *The Story of Siegfried*. He went on to write and edit more than 50 more.

L Frank Baum
1856–1919
Lyman Frank Baum was best known for creating the wonderful land of Oz. He came up with the name when he saw a filing cabinet labelled O–Z.

Thomas Frederick Crane
1844–1927
American Thomas Frederick Crane worked as a lawyer and academic, but devoted much of his spare time to collecting folklore.

Charles Dickens
1812–1870
Author of many famous novels, Charles Dickens' work includes *David Copperfield*. This book is based on his own childhood, when he had to leave school at the age of 12 to work in a factory.

Mrs Ewing
1841–1885
From a young age, Juliana Ewing wrote stories for children. Her husband was an army major, and she moved frequently, spending two years in Canada.

William Elliot Griffis
1843–1928
Both a minister and an author, William Elliot Griffis spent several years teaching in Japan. He wrote over 50 books, including many collections of fairy stories.

Nathaniel Hawthorne
1804–1864
Well-known author Nathaniel Hawthorne was a shy man, but made many friends. The novel *Moby-Dick* was dedicated to him.

Joseph Jacobs
1854–1916
Born in Australia, Joseph Jacobs became a distinguished folklorist, making several collections of fairy stories from England, Wales, Scotland, Europe and India.

E Pauline Johnson
1861–1913

Canadian Emily Pauline Johnson was the daughter of a Mohawk chief and an English settler. She made her living as a poet, storyteller and performer.

Charles Kingsley
1819–1875

An English clergyman, Charles Kingsley wrote many books, including *The Water Babies* and *Westward Ho!*, which gave its name to a town in Devon, UK.

Andrew Lang
1844–1912

Author and collector of fairy tales, Andrew Lang's *Blue Fairy Book* was a huge success and was followed by a further 11 books in the series.

Hamilton W Mabie
1846–1916

Hamilton Wright Mabie's parents wanted him to be a lawyer, but although he passed his exams with success, he hated law and became a journalist and author instead.

Sophia Morrison
1859–1917

Born on the Isle of Man, UK, Sophia Morrison worked there all her life to preserve its literature, music, language and folklore.

E Nesbit
1858–1924

Edith Nesbit wrote magical children's books. She once described herself as a child disguised by a grown-up's body.

Howard Pyle
1853–1911

American Howard Pyle was best-known as a writer and illustrator of traditional stories, such as tales of Robin Hood and King Arthur.

Katharine Pyle
1863–1938

Born into a warm and creative Quaker household, Katharine Pyle worked all her life as a writer and illustrator, like her brother, Howard.

Flora Annie Steel
1847–1929

Spending 22 years living in India, Flora Annie Steel involved herself in all sorts of projects, including acting as a school inspector and collecting local folklore.

Egerton R Young
1840–1909

A Methodist minister, Egerton Ryerson Young worked as a missionary with his wife among Native American tribes, and wrote books about his experiences.

About the Artists

Andy Catling works from his home in Hampshire, UK. He specializes in children's illustration, but has also produced digital artwork and animation for video games. Andy likes to lend his humour and sense of character to stories with historical and fairy tale themes. He is the proud owner of a messy work table and an excessive number of brushes.

Robert Dunn grew up with a keen interest in comics, books and horror films. He studied Fine Art at college, then found his vocation in children's illustration. Robert creates images with watercolour and pencil, and then adds the finishing touches digitally. He has worked on classic fiction collections, picture books and magazines. Robert lives in Scotland and is currently working on his own picture book.

Gerald Kelley works from his studio in Denver, Colorado, USA. He began working in watercolour and pencil, but now works digitally, from sketch to finished artwork. Illustrators Arthur Rackham and Edmund Dulac are major inspirations in Gerald's work. He loves illustrating fantastical tales and scary stories. Most days, Gerald can be found working busily at his screen.

Sara Sanchez has always had a passion for creativity. As a child, she would draw everything around her. Sara produces her illustrations using both traditional and digital techniques. She lives in Madrid, Spain, and works from her studio, where she enjoys spending hours creating her work.